THE NEW BIZARRO AUTHOR SERIES

PRESENTS

Uncle Sam's Carnival of Copulating Inanimals

KIRK JONES

Eraserhead Press
Portland, OR

THE NEW BIZARRO AUTHOR SERIES
An Imprint of Eraserhead Press

ERASERHEAD PRESS
205 NE BRYANT
PORTLAND, OR 97211

WWW.ERASERHEADPRESS.COM

ISBN: 1-936383-25-X

You hold in your hands now a book from the New Bizarro Author Series. Normally, Eraserhead Press publishes twelve books a year. Of those, only one or two are by new writers. The NBAS alters this dynamic, thus giving more authors of weird fiction a chance at publication.

For every book published in this series, the following will be true: This is the author's first published book. We're testing the waters to see if this author can find a readership, and whether or not you see more Eraserhead Press titles from this author is up to you.

The success of this author is in your hands. If enough copies of this book aren't sold within a year, there will be no future books from the author published by Eraserhead Press. So, if you enjoy this author's work and want to see more in print, we encourage you to help him out by writing reviews of his book, telling your friends, and giving feedback at www.bizarrocentral.com.

In any event, hope you enjoy…

—Kevin L. Donihe, Editor

Acknowledgements

Many thanks to those who guided me along the path to publication by listening, critiquing, inspiring and supporting my endeavors: Professors Cindy Daniels & Jennifer Mitchell. Fellow Bizarros Rose OKeefe, Kevin Donihe and Carlton Mellick III. Family members Amanda and Willow Jones. Last but not least, friends Jon Adams & Ken Peabody.
...this one's for Bones.

Chapter 1: Incarnation

Those who cared to peruse the historical records of Gary Olstrom, now known as the man made of tears, might observe that an extended streak of bad luck began for him, ironically, with a stroke of good luck at age eight, i.e. acquiring a position at the American Dollar, a hardware supply store in his hometown of Fine, NY. The streak of bad luck wasted no time in dispensing itself. For, on the first day of Gary's employment, he was asked by the owner to suspend a full-length mirror from the ceiling in the display area. It was this mirror that subsequently shattered, costing Gary his first paycheck. But before shattering, the action that seemed to perturb both Gary and his boss, Mr. Wakefield, significantly less was the separation of Gary's right arm from his shoulder.

It was not until Gary noticed the spatter of blood upon the now fragmented mirror that his squirming appendage neighboring said mirror became apparent. Gary turned his head and reflected calmly upon the surge of blood escaping his arm. Cupping the wound to the best of his ability, he jumped from the second step on the ladder and called to Mr. Wakefield. When his boss did not answer, he searched for him, covering the entire third isle of the store with blood and causing his neighbor, Mrs. Hemmingway, to die of shock.

When Mr. Wakefield finally came into view, he immediately presented Gary with a mop. "Now Gary," he explained, "you know our policy about work-related injuries, don't you?"

Gary, disappointed in himself, looked down at his feet.

"It was in the contract I made you sign. Do you remember?"

He shook his head.

"After we dress the wound you'll have to clean up isle three." Mr. Wakefield noted Mrs. Hemmingway's corpse strewn across the tiling. "Was she hurt in the accident, too?" he asked.

Again, Gary nodded.

Mr. Wakefield placed his hand on Gary's shoulder. "Very well. Wait in the back office. I'll be in momentarily to patch you up."

Were it not for Gary's calm disposition, it is likely he would have died from blood loss, but, after a short period of time, the gushing wound slowed to a trickle. Gary waited for his employer. Not more than five minutes later Mr. Wakefield returned, holding a small badge. He smiled cautiously. "Now, I know your parents are going to be upset. I never purchased any insurance for accidents such as these. So, in lieu of paying your medical bills, I'd like to present you with this purple badge of honor, for being wounded in the service of this fine establishment."

Gary bubbled with pride as he eyed the purple stock-paper heart, with crayon lettering declaring him a hero. "Mom and dad will be so proud," he mused, his stub's trickle flowing with greater persistence.

"Yes," Mr. Wakefield added. "You should probably head home to your folks. Looks like you're making more of a mess. I'll clean up here. It's the least I can do."

Upon arriving home, Gary beamed with pride, pointing with his remaining left arm at the purple heart he had been awarded. Father must have been quite proud, or so Gary suspected. For as soon as he walked through the door, father picked up the phone and dialed a number to proclaim his son's heroism to the entire town. This call was followed by the sound of sirens, and two state troopers whizzing past Gary's house, straight to Mr. Wakefield, who made his television debut later that evening, most likely for being such an honorable character, Gary imagined. What Gary couldn't figure out was why they showed footage of the state troopers extracting Mrs. Hemmingway's body from the dumpster behind American Dollar, nor why those silly officers would have put her there in the first place, only to rethink their decision and remove her again so quickly. At the very least, her family deserved a complimentary stock-paper purple heart such as the one Gary had acquired.

While local onlookers quipped at Gary's initial misfortune, it was not the loss of his arm, but the loss of his parents the following day that wrenched the purple heart from his chest. While the news of their fiery crash distressed him initially, he recovered a few days later when he discovered that their departure from this world was preceded by their visit to the orphanage for disabled children, where Gary was shipped the next day. There, he spent the remainder of his childhood years.

This tragedy was overshadowed by Gary's next occupation, his employment at a textile factory in Schenectady, New York at the age of 12. There, he learned the fine art of supervising other children and dodging insurance claims, just as his first hero, Mr. Wakefield, did. But upon re-spooling one of the nylon machines, Gary lost his footing, and, as a result, his right leg. Like many before him, his claim for compensation was denied, his employment terminated, and he was held fully responsible for cleaning his remnants. As he completed this final task, he was directed to a sign hanging above his machine. Apparently, one was supposed to turn it off before re-spooling. What nobody informed him was that one should also turn the machine off before cleaning blood from its inner-workings.

As some say, hindsight is 20/20. Unfortunately for Gary, this was not the case, because his second run-in with the nylon machine, even with the warning scrawled in red ink above him, rendered him blind in one eye. This was a minor loss, however, as he could never see, nor, for that matter, reason very well anyway.

After losing his job at the textile factory, Gary turned to the streets, struggling to attain sustenance and mental well-being. Several times, he believed he had found the proverbial foot in the door, only to realize that he had no right foot, nor a right leg, on which to stand. For a short while, he collected change on the subway while dancing upon a peg leg he forged from an old aluminum bucket and an oak cane he stole from a blind man in the gutter. But this eventually proved too tiresome for someone now entering his late teens, and thus Gary again wandered the streets aimlessly.

Then, one day, he found himself in the presence of a young man with similar handicaps: both a missing leg and a missing arm. But this man could afford sympathies. Gary soon found that was not all he could afford. Upon their second time crossing paths, the man offered Gary several dollars for food.

The third time the man limped by, Gary finally summoned the courage to ask, "Sir, by what means do you sustain yourself?"

"I'm employed by Uncle Sam, at the furniture factory," the man replied.

"Would it be possible for me to acquire a job with him as well?" Gary asked.

The man looked doubtful. "Come with me tomorrow and we shall see," he said, explaining, "I was in full health when I began working for him, and have been allowed to stay on due to seniority. Otherwise, I'd likely be accompanying you in the gutter. But I might be able to get you in. Meet me in front of the factory tomorrow." The man took a pen from his pocket, scrawled something on a small piece of paper and handed it to Gary. "Here's the address."

That evening, Gary prepared for his prospective job by stealing a razorblade from an inebriated subway drug addict and shaving. For the first time since his stay at the orphanage, Gary again saw his child-like visage splashed across a mirror. He wept for his own humanity, for his perseverance through poverty and the fact he had refused, on some level, to acknowledge his pain until the prospect that it might diminish arrived. All of these things ran through his mind as he journeyed to the factory so he could meet the mysterious man there bright and early. He promised himself he'd escape to an alleyway after catching a glimpse of the factory, but soon fell asleep against the gates.

The next morning, Gary was startled to waking by his armless, legless friend. Joyously, Gary extended his hand to be helped to his foot, but upon shifting his weight, found himself holding nothing more than a bloody stump. He screamed, but only a dull ringing persisted in his ears. His eyes darted from side to side, searching for explanation, until they found an answer in the mangled mass upon the ground, and the bus grinding to a halt before it.

But as luck would have it, the man was not quite dead. Gary tried to clear the ringing from his ears so he might hear the man's last request. But the man had only enough energy to graze the skyline with his eyes. Gary stayed with the man until life left him, feigning intimacy as he groped his coat for identification, eventually resolving to claim the garment for his own before the paramedics arrived. Its contents included a work ID and a curious vial of fluid marked "Regenagent #32." Being the Good Samaritan that he was, Gary decided to tell Henry's employer of the untimely tragedy.

* * *

When Gary entered the factory, he intended to request permission to visit the manager. Instead, a stout man standing just inside the door scolded him. "Henry! Get your ass up to Edward's Office! Christ, can't you hobble in on time for once?"

Gary headed upstairs and, opening the door to Edward's office, found the man mid-struggle with a disembodied arm. The limb pulled at his face and slapped maniacally against his back. "Get it off!" Edward shouted.

Gary ran to his assistance, pulling the flailing arm from the man's head and casting it to the floor.

"What the hell was that all about!?" Edward demanded.

Gary shrugged. "How am I supposed to know?"

"That was a test subject for your Regenagent," Edward explained, shuffling through papers. "Test #32. But what the hell was it doing?"

"I'd have to review the documents," Gary replied.

"You submitted the documents yesterday, Henry! I reapplied the agent ten minutes ago. Not long thereafter, the test subject crawled from its container and tried to kill me!" He paused for breath. "Was that *your* arm, by the way?"

Gary shook his head.

"Well, hunt the damned thing down! Make sure nobody sees it. Then we'll discuss your new lacquer, at length."

Gary fingered the vial in his coat pocket and complied, following the sound of startled workers in his search for the arm, which led him to the scrap room, equipped with two shredders and a compactor to make chipboard from obsolete and broken models. He found the arm at the compactor, taunting a man trapped inside the machine. He shouted desperately for help.

Gary rushed to the compactor, and the arm withdrew. As he turned from side to side to locate it, he felt it pull at the back of his head, smashing his face against the compression button repeatedly until the man inside was crushed. It took all of Gary's strength to recoil from the series of blows, so much strength, in fact, that the force sent both Gary and the arm backwards into the neighboring wood chipper, which was, at the moment, running full bore.

Falling head first into the chipper didn't give Gary much

time to contemplate his fate. In fact, upon recollection, his last memory was of slipping backwards. Or was he pulled by the thread of his coat? He couldn't remember. All he knew was that the initial blow was followed by a searing pain that prompted tears. What he didn't know was that one of those tears, as fate would have it, coalesced on the scrap room floor with the contents of the small vial of Regenagent #32 in his coat pocket.

* * *

Uncle Sam shifted in his chair and placed his feet upon his desk. It occurred to him that his legs were not unlike darning needles, with softball kneecaps inflamed from rheumatoid arthritis. *These damned things*, he thought as he ran his fingers across a complex myriad of varicose veins. Like Braille, the network of lightning lines and throbbing clusters seemed to communicate to him. They said, "Remove us. Better yet, do away with the whole lot. Lose the legs, Sam."

He reached for a cooler at his side, extracting a packet of dry ice. He lifted his pant leg dutifully and placed the dry ice upon a particularly knotted group of veins. "It burns!" he shouted.

A knock at the door.

Sam returned the packet to the cooler and closed the lid quickly. "What is it?" he asked.

"May I enter?" the meager voice on the other side requested.

"Yes," he replied.

Uncle Sam's assistant, Bob, peeked in. "A small problem, sir, in the scrap room."

"Can't you handle it? I'm supposed to pick up my niece at the airport."

"Not this time, sir. It's pressing," Bob said, adding, "I could pick her up for you if you'd prefer."

"No, that'll be fine." Sam kicked the cooler of dry ice under his desk. "What'd you say the problem was?"

"You'd better check for yourself."

"I'm too old for this fucking job. When do you think they'll let me retire, Bob?"

"You're the boss, sir."

Sam rose from his chair. "Hardly."

Chapter 2: Inglorious Rebirth

Gary woke that afternoon in the scrap room, lacking a body completely. Invisible, he could still feel his nerve endings. His entire fleshless being stung like a ghost appendage after amputation. He sulked, wondering if he would ever again interact with another person. As he put what felt like his hands to his non-existent face, he noticed a gelatinous substance coalescing with his aura, the source of which, from what he could tell, was his immaterial eyes. Soon, the translucent substance encompassed the ebb and flow of his energies. His elation prompted yet more tears, which in turn prompted more of the substance to accumulate. And as he cried a complete body of vitreous humor, first with tears of sorrow followed by tears of joy, an anonymous voice squelched his fear of forever being alone. Uncle Sam had entered to the sound of these tears. "Why are you crying, young man?" he asked.

Gary turned to see a thin, aging man, garbed in red and blue with a beard of white. He opened his mouth, tried to speak. His lungs bubbled, producing only a faint gurgling sound. If, however, Gary had been able to speak, he would have said, "I weep because I have nobody to love. I have no heart with which to love. I have no brain and no courage. I'm like a gelatinous medley of L. Frank Baum's outcast characters, with no Judy Garland with which to share the pain."

"That's exactly why I am here," Sam said.

In time, Gary found his voice. "You understood me?" he asked.

"Yes, and I, like you, am a living being composed of something other than flesh. I too am translucent, or rather, a mirage," he said, "but of a different consistency: false promises, broken dreams, the tears of those orphaned and anally intruded upon by my mother, Capitalism. I am America incarnate."

"But you look so clean, so perfect."

"That is the nature of illusion," the man explained. "May I ask your name?"

"Gary."

The tall man stroked his beard. "Nice to meet you, Gary. They call me Uncle Sam," he said. "I run this place. Did you work for me?"

In the midst of confusion, Gary shook his head.

"Perhaps you might consider doing so now. If you will join me, and my carnival, you will find that you too are perfect, or at least you appear to be, which in society's eyes is all that matters. Our people feed off illusion, Gary."

"Carnival?"

"Indeed." Sam extended his hand.

Gary reached out, his hand slipping through Uncle Sam's when they touched.

"I guess you'll have to get to your feet on your own. Come with me," he said, pulling a cell phone from his pocket. He dialed quickly, raising a finger to pause their conversation. "Yes. Bob," he said. "Could you clean up the wood chipper for me? I'll lock up as I leave." He paced as he spoke. "Yes. Yes, it's quite a mess. No, you should not file an insurance claim on his behalf."

Gary noticed Sam's shadow change form as it grazed the Regenagent #32 on the floor. It appeared as if encompassed by a flame, which then fragmented into hundreds of little worm-like appendages that snaked up the walls and out of the room.

"Oh," Sam added, "Looks like I'll need you to pick up my niece at the airport after all. I'm going back to the carnival." He rolled his eyes. "Yes, you can bring her there." He closed his phone and placed it back in his pocket. "Sorry for the interruption, young man. Follow me."

They walked a short distance to a door neighboring the scrap room. Sam toggled with the doorknob and followed Gary past the threshold. Inside the room, a large network of wires lined the floor. "I've been involved in this carnival for years. The furniture factory is just a front and a source of income to fund my experiments. My first endeavor was the creation of a portable HAARP device to control the weather. Here's where it all began." Sam reached for a control panel near the doorway, activated the device. Wires on the floor buzzed and crackled. "This one's designed to interfere with analog communications, but I designed my portable model to alter weather patterns as well. You need good weather to run a carnival."

He turned off the machine. "My second undertaking was to create something that would imbue any object with a soul. I have found success with certain serums developed by my employees, though they only work on inanimate objects." He continued, "Once the objects come into contact with the serum, they become living creatures, so to speak. They can communicate, but only by means with which they are naturally adorned. For example, a desk or chair could scrape across the ground in certain ways to express emotions, but few, if any, can communicate using written or spoken language. There was a man who taught a coffee pot some utterances, but who is to say that means anything at all?"

Gary was confused, but found solace in the fact that Uncle Sam seemed to sense this and returned to more concrete observations:

"We call them inanimals," he explained. "One thing inanimals do well is copulate. They copulate wildly, and with conviction like no human could muster. A desk will fuck its counterpart to shambles. They can also be domesticated. They make wonderful pets. Would you like that, Gary? Would you like a pet to console and take care of?"

Gary nodded emphatically.

"Come with me then." Uncle Sam walked into the adjacent room. A large yellow curtain hung on the far side. "This is the doorway to your future." Sam yanked a cord. The yellow drapes pulled back, revealing a landscape of viscous white. Sam looked at Gary. "Let's go," he said.

Once through the wall, it was almost as if time had shifted them away from space. As they moved forward, air rippled like water until it stretched tight, shattered, and the dust-encrusted earth below became apparent. In the distance, Gary saw large Ferris wheels, which moved unlike any he had previously witnessed. Banana-colored tents dotted the bland landscape.

"Gary, this is my carnival."

They pressed onward, noting people scattered between the tents, carrying buckets and film equipment. In an otherwise deserted land, the carnival overflowed with life.

Sam laughed, waving to those who crossed his path as he approached the first tent with Gary. "Come," he insisted. "Witness what we do here."

The curtain parted to reveal several desks copulating before a young man garbed in traditional cowboy attire.

"This is my cameraman and couch whisperer, Ignatius," Uncle Sam said.

Gary extended his hand.

Ignatius put his camera down for a moment. "Are you talking to someone?" he asked.

Uncle Sam grazed a desktop until he found a blue marker, with which he drew a large X on Gary's chest. It quickly disappeared, absorbed into Gary's being, momentarily turning him the color of the sky as reflected in a clear body of water.

"Sorry," Ignatius said, extending his hand. "Didn't see you there."

Gary returned the gesture, slightly hurt, but understanding. While he again had a body, he was practically invisible.

"Ignatius films my inanimals for promotion across the country. You wouldn't think it, but furniture porn is a successful industry...or it was, anyway."

"We do it all," said Ignatius. "Desk-on-desk. Person-on-Desk. Desks-on-person orgies. Whatever you're into, we've got it."

The cameras continued to roll. One desk, stacked beneath two others, began to buckle. The aluminum legs bent inward and the wooden top cracked. Still, Ignatius filmed.

"They're killing it!" Gary shouted.

Sam bent down and whispered into Gary's ear. "Furniture doesn't have an orgasm. It stops once its partner has been completely obliterated. That's the closest thing to a climax furniture porn can simulate. It's harsh, but I promise you they can't feel a thing."

The desk finally collapsed on the floor as those on top ground to a halt. Though they didn't have discernable features with which to convey emotion, Gary thought they looked solemn.

"That black one," Uncle Sam said, pointing to a smaller desk. "He's frisky. You think he'd make a good pet, Gary?"

Gary shook his head. The vigorous performance of the desk had made him wary.

"Don't read violence into it," Uncle Sam said. "The damaged desks can be rebuilt. They're all good-natured."

Gary nodded.

Ignatius turned off the camera and approached the remaining furniture. "Good job, folks," he said. "I can scrub you down or re-stain, if you need." He nodded in the direction of Sam and Gary. "I better get back to it. Nice to meet you, Gary." He tipped his hat cordially. "If you'll excuse me."

Uncle Sam put his hand on Gary's back, applying little pressure so as to avoid sinking into Gary's being. "Come with me."

Once outside, Sam explained his predicament. "Gary,"

he said gently as he led him into another tent. "I'd be lying if I said that taking you in was merely an act of kindness. I've never seen anything like you before. We need you, Gary. Our industry's not as lucrative as it once was."

"What do you want me to do?" Gary asked.

"I'd like you to direct the inanimals in my circus. Ignatius works well behind the camera, but I need someone to help me when we take this show on the road, an inanimal tamer for the live shows. What do you say?"

"I'll try, I guess."

"We thought about breaking into the fetish market," Uncle Sam explained. "Then we considered expanding our repertoire of inanimals. But power tools, their form of communication is dangerous. Can't do knives without inevitable death, either. Furniture's about all we have. So we have to do something new for the old audience, or do the same old thing for a new one. I'm pushing for the latter." He handed Gary a small whip, nodded in the direction of two small chairs.

Gary reached for the whip, but it passed through his hands. He tried again and shook his head.

"Don't give up so easily," Sam said. "Focus."

Gary closed his eyes, visualized himself grabbing the whip. He tried once more, with success. Whip in hand, he approached the chairs. They seemed to cringe.

"Put the whip at your side, Gary. There's no need to frighten them unless they refuse to comply," Sam instructed. "You need only utter one of several commands. Stay, desist, copulate; those are the most important."

Gary lowered the whip. It slid through his hands and fell to the floor. He bent down, focused and picked it up. "Copulate," he demanded.

The two chairs turned towards one another, as if negotiating who would be the fucker and who the fuckee.

"They're very indecisive, Gary," Sam said. "The crowd won't wait for them to make up their own minds. 'Bottom' and 'top' are two additional commands you'll want to utilize. Simply point to the one you're addressing with your empty hand to address them individually."

Gary pointed to a small oak chair, figuring he was the sturdier of the two. "Bottom," he said.

The chair complied. The other, a small antique white three-legged chair, followed suit, mounting its oaken counterpart.

"That's exactly what we're looking for. *You're* exactly what we're looking for. Hell, maybe someday you'll even take over my position. Run this carnival for yourself." Sam pulled a cigar out of his pocket, lit it and inhaled deeply. "Do you understand?"

"I do," Gary replied, and he did. When Gary had only partially reconstituted as vitreous humor, it was the painful memories of his past—of his longing to again be a part of society—that caused him to move forward. With the help of Uncle Sam, he could move forward *and* reintegrate with society. The principle seemed honorable, if not personally beneficial.

"Then you'll join us?" Sam asked.

"I will."

Chapter 3: The Long Journey

The following morning, Gary woke to Uncle Sam shouting in the distance. Gary followed the voice until he saw Sam directing the others to pack for their journey. A young brunette accompanied him. She had shoulder-length hair and eyes as empty and black as Gary's heart had felt since his reconstitution.

"Gary!" Sam called. "Come here!"

As Gary closed in on Sam and his female companion, he couldn't help but feel envious. *No doubt his money and charisma plays part in procuring a woman so young*, he thought. *Perhaps she's just a friend.*

Sam walked to meet him. The young woman trailed close behind. "Today's the day, Gary," he said. "Are you ready?"

Gary smiled. Of course he was ready. He had been since the dawn of his invisibility.

"I'd like you to meet my niece, Liberty. She just arrived this morning."

She came closer.

Were her eyes brown, black?

Neither. They were, in fact, not there at all.

She tucked her hair behind her ear. "Nice to meet you," she said.

Gary stood dumbfounded, deterred by her empty eye sockets and confused by his continued attraction towards her.

"Gary," Uncle Sam prodded.

"Nice to meet you," he said, reaching out to shake her hand.

Before Gary had time to savor the gentle caress of her fingers, Uncle Sam pulled him away, leading him to the rear of the carnival convoy. "Bye," Gary shouted. Liberty waved daintily.

"Please do not be offended," Uncle Sam began as he

showed Gary to the last cart. "Ignatius and the others have requested that you remain in the rear. If you want a position at the front of the convoy, you'll have to earn it. All in due time, my boy."

"Will you keep me company?" Gary asked.

Uncle Sam shook his head. "I'm afraid not. We'll all eat together, however, when we make our first stop. Where is your pet, son?"

Gary anxiously scrutinized the landscape.

Uncle Sam smiled. "Don't worry. He must be in the front. I'll call him back for you. Akimbo!" he shouted. "Akimbo! Here pup!"

Gary was shocked to find the black desk he initially met had been re-stained a more pleasant color, a deep walnut brown revealing smoothed knots and the inner-workings of the original tree. It gave the desk character.

Uncle Sam patted the desk on its top. "Would you like to join Gary?" he asked.

The desk stamped its feet on the ground in a sort of desk-speak, the frequency of which implied "hell yes!"

The caravan started moving about an hour after Gary found a seat at the rear of the convoy. It seemed unfair, since even the giant bureau, the eight-foot mirror, and the small chicken coop were housed in separate carts before him. The convoy was long, and Gary wondered how many carts were between Uncle Sam and himself.

Like the convoy, the trip was long, too. Gary wiled away the hours playing games with Akimbo, such as "clap the rhythm," in which Gary would slap his vitreous humor hands together in a sequence that Akimbo would then be expected to repeat by stamping the ground with his forelegs. Akimbo was quite adept at the game, and this amused Gary to no end.

* * *

Later that day, they arrived on the outskirts of the city, which, for Gary, was reminiscent of a cacophony of machines not unlike the rainforest utterances of birds and other animals, the hisses of hydraulics like cicadas under banana leaves. Despite the noise, the skyline was surprisingly still.

Ignatius helped Akimbo out of the trailer. Gary followed, using Akimbo as a stool of sorts as Ignatius scratched his head. "No time to reflect on the city's beauty," he said. "We have work to do...uhh. Well shit, I can't rightly think of no chore you can do without getting your gooey...what the hell are you made of, boy?" He dropped his hands to his side, forsook the possibility of response in haste. "You ever rake shit?"

Gary shook his head.

Ignatius handed him a shovel. "Just scrape all the shit out of the caravans onto the ground here. Then we'll move the carts into the city limits this afternoon."

Gary took the shovel and began his chore with a diligence not matched since his first job with Mr. Wakefield. But each time Gary's mind wandered from the chore, the shovel slipped through his hands. This happened several times before he focused his will on holding it. He realized then that even the most menial of tasks required full concentration, which allowed little time for daydreaming and fantasy.

* * *

That evening, the townspeople gathered, entering one of the bright yellow tents for Uncle Sam's Carnival. The show was about to begin.

Behind the curtain, Uncle Sam, Ignatius, Gary and Liberty waited anxiously. "Are you ready, Gary?" Uncle Sam asked. "I know you're nervous, but do you think you can do it? The couches are larger than the small chairs you trained when we first met, but, in principle, everything works the same."

Gary was unsure. He looked upon the people, the yellow light glazing them, casting a jaundiced look upon the many expectant fans. "I'll try," he said.

The lights dimmed. Uncle Sam parted the curtain, which, to Gary, looked like a bright yellow vagina emblazoned with large red stars. He exited through the curtains with this image in mind, lowered the whip to his side and commanded the two large couches. "Desist!" he shouted. The couches' playful disposition immediately transitioned to what Gary perceived as fear. He pointed to one of the two couches, large and purple-velvet. He weighed the two items against one another in his mind, determining that the purple-velvet couch was the sturdiest. "Bottom," he commanded.

From behind the curtain, Uncle Sam, Liberty and Ignatius watched. "What's he doing?" Liberty asked.

Ignatius began, "He takes those two couches, and—"

"Let me tell her," Sam interrupted. Gently, he placed his hand on her shoulder. "He tames our inanimals. Teaches them tricks."

"That's fascinating!" she replied. "I never knew you led such an interesting life, Uncle."

"Your mother never spoke of me?"

"Rarely." She turned back to the spectacle, wide-socketed, a smile on her face.

In the center of the tent, Gary's performance continued. The purple couch braced itself as the other, a smaller, white polyester model, prepared to mount. With little to no effort on Gary's behalf, the act had begun. Gasps filled the air as patrons vomited in ecstasy, making their way to the troughs at the front of the tent.

One man's shouts, interspersed with sounds of his convulsing esophagus, led him to uncontrollable spasms on the floor.

Another man stuck his finger down his throat to prompt

a purge, but upon failure, shrugged and ran for the trough, diving in headfirst, sliding all the way to the other end as fans puked with glee at the sight of Gary's act.

Gary was shocked. Never before had he seen such proclivities up close. Suddenly, he saw the purple velvet couch buckling under the pressure of its partner, and realized the show was almost over. He noted the couch cushions bouncing up and down, too. *Please don't ask for an encore*, he thought to himself as he prepared to direct the couches backstage. *Please don't ask for an encore*. And, as he raised his whip to order that the couches desist, the audience shouted, "More! More!" As if sensing this, the white polyester couch resisted.

Gary struggled to pull the couches apart. Finally, the white couch, perturbed by Gary's interference, slowed its pace, dismounted and rushed its master. Gary raised the whip, trying his best to avoid the couch's advance, but to no avail. In its urgency, the couch toppled him.

Ignatius was first on the scene, pulling Gary from the floor. "Christ, Gary, you could have been killed!" he said. "Down!" he shouted as the couch recoiled. "Down!"

"Is everything ok?" Liberty asked.

"It's fine," Sam replied.

"I thought they were harmless?" Gary asked as he was dragged from the center stage.

"As long as you don't provoke them," he explained. "I told Sam you shouldn't be allowed out here without proper training!"

As the crowd erupted with cheers and vomit once more, Gary reflected on the fact that their entertainment nearly came at the cost of his life.

"Show's over," Sam said. "Bob, turn off the lights. Take Liberty to her sleeping quarters."

"But I want to congratulate Gary," she insisted.

"Tomorrow, dear."

"Come," Bob said coolly. "We don't want to upset your Uncle."

* * *

After the show, Sam invited the performers into his private tent for payout. Gary happily accepted the meager sum Sam offered. But when Sam offered Ignatius money for handling the inanimals, he dashed the compensation from his hand. "I told you, Sam!" he shouted. "Desks is one thing, but you can't trust the new guys with big furniture!"

"Gary's alright," Sam remarked. "I'm sure he could have handled himself."

But Ignatius saw the repellant frown as Uncle Sam approached Gary from behind. He grabbed Sam's arm. "You don't give a damn about nobody but yourself!"

Sam pushed Ignatius towards the door. "I made you, Ignatius, brought you from the bottom up. Could have been anyone. Could have been Bob." He smiled coyly. "Could have been old Gary here."

"You can't replace me, Sam! You ain't never gonna find another couch whisperer as good as I am and you know it!"

Ignatius stormed from the room, with Gary following slowly behind him.

"Gary," Sam called. "Pay no attention to him. He gets upset like this every time someone new enters the circus. He's just jealous."

Still, Gary walked from tent to tent until he saw Ignatius near the stalls.

"Just go away," Ignatius said, waving his hand dismissively.

Gary turned to leave.

"Wait, don't go," Ignatius said. "You know, sometimes when I get lonely, I come out here near these outhouse contraptions. Something about that lingering scent of fresh shit mingling with the open range, those lights in the distance.

Ah hell, I love it here! But I just...I gotta leave this fandangled carnival."

"But you said it yourself," Gary reasoned. "You're the only couch whisperer."

"Damn it, Gary! Could you just not worry about Uncle Sam and this goddamned rodeo carnival bullshit? You damn near got yourself killed out there today. And for what? So a few people could watch you make a man-eating couch fuck another?"

"It's more than that," Gary said. "Those people shared something tonight."

Ignatius rose from his stoop and grabbed Gary by the shoulders, his hands sinking in deep. "You need to prioritize, boy. Uncle Sam don't give two shits about how they feel, or how any of us feel for that matter. Social veneer's his social veneer. He's just coverin' shit with honey."

Gary looked frightened. Bilious vitreous humor swirled in his eyes, soon trickling down his face like urine in a subway gutter. It was the first trace of emotion Ignatius had witnessed in those near-invisible eyes. Then Gary pushed away, turning towards the inanimal cages. As he continued walking, he heard Ignatius' voice, trailing across the range like a coyote howling to its mate in the night. "Gary, you need to stay out of the pen with those damned couches if you don't know what's goin' on. But I can help you before I leave." Ignatius ran to catch him.

"Really, you can't leave," Gary said.

Ignatius embraced him. "Don't cry."

"I'm not. It's just that Uncle Sam needs you, and—"

"I know saying goodbye is hard," he interrupted. "I'll stick around until I can teach you my ways. Shouldn't take long."

"I barely know you, Ignatius."

"No, Gary," he said. "I won't hear none of it." Ignatius stepped away and dried his own eyes. "Let's get down to business."

* * *

The next morning Gary rose, all the memories from the previous night still fresh in his mind. His crash course in couch whispering had been a success. Never show fear. Patience is a virtue. Those were two of the many rules and aphorisms Ignatius imparted to Gary.

"Anything else?" Gary had asked.

"Yeah," Ignatius had said. "Carry this here taser. It ain't for you and I to determine whether or not them sons a bitches got emotions. And they might not feel much, but 10,000 volts will just about knock them back to the furniture farm they came from."

Gary expected to see Ignatius that morning for a final test run. But all he found was a letter stapled to the outer canvas of his cart.

Gary,

Our time together was short and true, but just like a small penis, that don't mean it's any less efficient as acting like a dowsin' rod for pussy, no matter what a woman tells you. You might not think you are, but you're ready. You got the gift, Gary. You can understand the jibber jabber o' those goddanged inanimate objects. That's why Akimbo took such a likin' to ya.

By the way, left the morning's newspaper in front of your tent. Looks like you were all the rage.

Love,
Ignatius.

Gary sighed as he bored a hole into his chest with his thumb and embedded the letter therein, sealing it over for later viewing. A second later, he felt the all-knowing hand of Uncle Sam upon his shoulder. "Ignatius," Gary said, turning. "He's gone."

"He's been on his way out for a long time. Come on, son. Let's pack up for the next city and get that HAARP running. Looks like a storm is coming."

Gary carried out his chores as taught to him by his superiors: clean the pens, polish the desks, etc. In a relatively short time, he found himself in the back of the caravan with Akimbo.

As they cleared out, Gary saw the storm approaching. Lightning crept through the purple backdrop, wiping the horizon clean of color as a dust-brush blew across their path, erasing all evidence of their travels.

Chapter 4: Another Time, Another Place

By that evening, Gary could see Philadelphia on the horizon. Aside from the glaze of dusk, Philly was a relatively colorless place, but pleasantly so: the sun almost finding its way through the mesh of gray, the winds gentle enough to sift dust rather than ejaculate it into one's pores. In its own strange way, it was beautiful.

When they stopped to set up camp that evening, Uncle Sam again approached Gary's caravan, and with a hand perched upon Gary's shoulder, guided his eyes across the skyline as an astronomer might guide one's eyes across the zodiac.

"Over there's the old prison," Sam said, pointing to a small light towering above the others. "The Panopticon, a symbol of solidarity against lawlessness. It gives people reassurance that crime is under control. On a figurative level, that old prison's always at odds with the newspapers."

"Sounds like any prison to me," Gary said.

"She's stratified vertically, has a new setup so many can be observed by one. They called it innovation. I just call it the polar opposite of a carnival tent. Instead of everybody on the outside looking in, it's one man on the inside, looking at everybody on the outside. It's all perspective, Gary. Relative, you know?"

He paused, waiting for an answer. Gary said nothing.

"You know, isolation probably wouldn't be quite so bad if people saw themselves as the man on the inside rather than the man on the outside looking in. We'd all be the leader of our own little world. Wouldn't that be nice?"

"Who would we lead it for?" Gary asked.

"Come on, Gary," Sam said. "Time for bed. Tomorrow's going to be an important performance."

* * *

The next morning, Gary woke to the sound of inanimals stirring in their carts. He rose from bed and stepped out of the caravan into the light of day.

Bob approached with several unbound scrolls in his hand. "Gary!" he shouted. "Uncle Sam asked me to bring these to you!"

Gary looked down at parchment as Bob unraveled one. It read: *Tonight! Gary the amazing inanimal tamer and his cataclysmic couches!*

"Looks like your reputation precedes you this time," Bob observed as he handed another of the folded papers to him. Gary opened a second flyer. Inside, there was a thumbnail print of Gary rendered in black ink. Though blotchy, the image captured him squatting before a black smudge, which he assumed was a couch.

Gary poked another hole in his right butt cheek and, upon hollowing it out a few inches in diameter, folded the flyer and inserted it therein for safe keeping. He then proceeded with his chores. He gathered the rake from caravan four, just as Ignatius had once instructed, and started for the inanimal cages.

During Gary's training, Ignatius warned that he must always start with the large inanimals first: "They're the hardest to control, but trust me, you'd much rather have one bureau out of control than a herd of chairs. If we could, we'd pen 'em, but that's too much setup. That's why we park the trailers in a circle, to keep the inanimals in. Containment's important. But remember, the little ones can slip through the cracks. You have to watch them closely. So get the big ones out first. And don't forget the taser."

Gary extracted the taser from a pouch of vitreous humor on his waist and opened the door to the two couches first. "Come on girls, er, boys...whatever the hell you are."

The couches stumbled out gently, revealing behind them a footrest.

Gary marveled at the addition. *I don't recall loading that up on the way*, he thought.

Though confused, he trudged onward. All was as it should be, until he reached the desks' trailer. When he uncovered them, he found not ten, but thirty or more desks all stacked upon one another, some of which had collapsed at the bottom of the cage.

"Uncle Sam!" Gary shouted.

There was no reply. He walked to Sam's cart, entering without a second thought. "Sir, the inanimals are reproducing."

Inside, Sam meticulously packed dry ice around his legs. "If you need assistance, call to Bob!" He continued rearranging the containers around his legs. "Uncle Sam, Uncle Sam!" he droned mockingly. "It takes a good hour to pack my legs in dry ice, and every fucking time I finish there's some problem with factory operations, or the caravan, or *something*." He continued, "Uncle Sam, a wheel broke on one of the carts. Uncle Sam, the bureau is keeping the desks up. Uncle Sam, one of our hands is bleeding to death. God!"

"I—I'll leave you to your business then, sir. Just thought you should know."

"Thank you. Leave. Now."

Gary closed the door behind him, drenching the room in shadow once more.

* * *

Sam waited until he could no longer hear Gary's footsteps on the stairs. "Are you still there?"

"Yessssssssss," the shadows seemed to reply.

"Why can't you reveal yourselves to me?"

"We are all around you."

Sam peered at the walls cautiously, looking for the voice's source. "You're the shadows, the darkness?"

"You haven't noticed?" they whispered. "The Regenagent on the factory floor. She gave us life. We're your shadow."

"What do you want?"

The shadows shifted on the walls, producing varying degrees of darkness. "To help."

Sam cocked an eyebrow. "You want to perform?"

"In our own way, yes."

"Well, I could use some assistance testing the Regenagent."

"Bodies," the chorus erupted in whispers. "You need bodies."

Sam wasn't sure he'd heard them right. "I'd like to determine its potency," he continued, "see if we can make a more concentrated serum."

"You need bodies," the chorus reiterated, this time quite clearly, "souls, to determine the Regenagent's reach."

"While you have a point, I can't afford any more blood on my hands right now."

"In cities like Philadelphia, half of the people are invisible. Nobody will notice."

Sam folded his hands together, thought for a moment. "Alright," he said. "But be careful, okay?"

But while the room remained dark, the shadows were gone.

* * *

Gary rushed to the smallest tent, which was currently being erected. "Bob," he said, catching his breath. "Do these things reproduce?"

"We pick up a few strays in every city," Bob replied. "But as for reproducing, I've never seen the likes."

Gary waved him back towards the couches.

"Well I'll be damned," Bob said. "I haven't seen a footrest

in a long time. Another stray?"

"It can't be a stray. I packed only couches in before we left New York. Something's wrong."

Bob inspected the neighboring cage of desks. "Looks like there's a few more in here, too. Well, there's no use in worrying too much about a good thing. We'll sell the broken ones off as scrap, and maybe we can sell a few as pets tonight."

"How're we going to keep track of all of them?" Gary asked.

"Doesn't matter, as long as we have ten desks and two couches for the show."

"But they aren't trained."

"They're tame enough," Bob replied.

"You want me to let them out, then?"

"Yeah, let them roam for a bit. They'll be fine. I gotta finish the tent, unless you want to switch jobs?"

Gary shook his head and began to unlatch the desk cage. But, as soon as he opened the door, the pressure forced the desks outward and onto Gary. The desks scurried through the threshold, trampling him underfoot. By the time they were done, Gary's gooey flesh had adhered to the ground. "Uncle Sam won't like this," he said.

Just then, he heard the child-like laughter of a girl behind him: Liberty.

"Gary?" She approached and reached out to help him to his feet. "Sounds like you have a lot of picking up to do around here."

"It's pretty obvious, isn't it?" Gary said, extending his arms to present the mess.

"It sounded bad. But I can't see, remember? How bad is it?"

Gary noticed that Liberty was ankle-deep in his right calf. "Terrible." He reached down to help clear the debris and fell again to the ground.

She laughed playfully. "Don't worry," she said. "I'll take

care of it. You get back to work."

Gary tugged at his calf, reattached it to his knee and walked away, rather embarrassed. The only consolation was her reply as he left:

"Look forward to hearing the show tonight."

He wanted to smile, turn back and wave. Anything. But the humiliation was too great. Though she couldn't see, she had felt and heard him make an ass of himself. He recalled hearing somewhere that when one lost a sense, other senses were amplified to compensate. *I must have sounded like a fool*, he thought.

* * *

That evening, Gary parted the curtains to a crowd much larger than before. Quickly, he closed the curtain and withdrew into his paranoid imagination.

Sam, sensing his anxieties, urged him on. "Come on, Gary. You can do it."

Gary remembered those gaping chasms that were the eyeholes of Liberty. He felt he could tuck his love therein like one of the many makeshift holes in his body; never had he seen a woman so beautiful. He closed his eyes, thought of her and walked onto the floor.

Some ridiculed and mocked him, but between the throbbing in his ears and the supportive cheers, Gary managed to block them out. He approached the center of the ring, groped the taser at his side. The inanimals, two couches, went from agile to lethargic. Gary ordered the larger of the two, a black pleather three-person, to the bottom, prompting the other to mount. But the purple velvet couch, this time to be positioned on top, refused to move.

The crowd fell silent, leaving only the sound of crying children. Some cried due to cotton candy embedded in their cavities. But most cried for Gary, for the fried bread dough and hot dog waiting to be discharged into the vomit troughs near the stands.

From behind the curtain, Liberty listened intently. Uncle Sam was nearby. "What's wrong with him?" she asked.

"The animals sense his self-doubt," Sam observed. "He'll be alright."

Gary thought of the children, and whipped the ground when he heard someone gagging in the stands. He turned. A tear ran down his cheek when he saw Ignatius, who had returned to watch the show. To prompt Gary into action, he made himself vomit. Others followed, and like the wave made so famous at previous sporting events, a cascade of puke fell upon each row, starting top center and working its way down.

Gary remembered the first time he held the whip. Since then, he had managed to pick up objects and shake hands with little to no effort. Gary wondered, since he could touch things with almost intangible fingers, maybe he could touch them with his consciousness, too. It was worth a shot. He tightened his hands into fists and focused. *Pease. Just do... what you're meant to do.* He nodded in their direction. *Please. Make love.*

It seemed Gary was getting through to the couches. But, before topping its partner, the purple one walked off stage. Carnival music in the background stopped abruptly, replaced by Marvin Gaye. The couch returned, edging towards its partner in synch with the music. It topped the black couch. The rhythm with which they copulated was significantly slower than that of the desks Gary had first witnessed. Just as he had asked, the couches were making love.

The crowd went wild.

After nearly half an hour, Gary heard the gurgling hum of the crowd dissipate. Turning, he again placed his hand on the taser, and the purple velvet couch dismounted. He bubbled with pride and bowed, unreserved for the first time.

Uncle Sam ran to his side, microphone in hand. "The amazing Gary!" He lowered the microphone. "I've never seen them act so tender towards one another. Goddamn boy, you're going to be a star!"

Gary half-listened as he searched the audience for Ignatius. When he could not find him, his eyes fell upon the ground. Gary noticed Sam no longer had a shadow as he guided him to the back.

Liberty was the first to greet him behind the curtain. "Oh Gary," she said, "that was beautiful!"

"Your best thus far," Bob said.

Liberty touched Gary. "But your arm... You've overexerted yourself with that whip."

"Maybe I have," he observed.

"Don't worry," Uncle Sam said. "Liberty's a medical aide. She'll help you fix that." Sam looked to Liberty and nodded in Gary's direction.

"Uncle, I'm not a medical—"

"—ridiculous," Sam interrupted. "You'll do as good a job as any, Liberty. Help Gary back to his cart."

* * *

Liberty carefully smoothed out Gary's arm with vitreous humor he'd collected in a bucket for such an occasion. "That feel alright?" she asked.

Gary flexed his arm, bent it at the elbow. "Fine," he said.

"The crowd seemed pretty enamored. How did you get the inanimals to act like that?"

Gary looked down and blushed. "I don't know. I just willed them to, I guess." He noticed Liberty's feet, turned inward, and her downcast glance between random eye-socket contact. "Liberty?" he asked.

"Yes?"

He responded by cradling her face with one hand, circling

her eye sockets with a finger on the opposite hand.

She pushed it away. "I can't," she said.

"What's wrong?"

"I've never been with a man before."

"Can I kiss you?" he asked.

She nodded, closed her sockets and waited.

But now he found himself reluctant, afraid.

Liberty eventually opened her eyes and headed for the door. "I should get back to my tent," she said.

Gary sat up, perplexed. "Did I do something wrong?"

She smiled. "Would you walk with me?"

"Of course."

As they stepped into the cool night, Liberty slid her hand into his. A lightning-like sensation coursed through his body. "You know, Gary, my uncle has big plans for you."

"I know," he mumbled.

"Sometimes my parents, they say what he's doing is wrong. Well, my mother used to anyway. She's gone now."

"What happened to her?"

"She died."

"I'm sorry." Gary paused, eager to change the subject, but unable to think of anything to discuss.

"You ever have doubts, about what you're doing in the carnival?"

"Not really, I—"

A scream, reverberating between the tents, cut short Gary's response. Liberty broke her grip and ran towards the sound.

She froze between the bureau and desk cages, and, when Gary arrived at her side, he knew why.

"Blood," Liberty said. "I can smell it."

A young woman, drenched in shadow, lay at the edge of the bureau's cage. As liberty knelt at her side and checked her pulse, the shadows appeared to disperse. "She's dead. Get Uncle Sam."

Gary ran to Uncle Sam's tent. It was empty. Gary would have to go into town himself to notify the proper authorities.

* * *

He stumbled through dimly-lit alleys, bent on contacting the first man in uniform, or the first man beating a civilian of lower status, as both signified an officer in a city where there weren't as many uniforms as there were eyes. When he found neither brutality nor uniforms, Gary settled on searching for the suspicious and weathered gaze of a detective. But, as Gary meandered onward, it occurred to him that everyone cast a suspicious glance, save those who recognized Gary from Uncle Sam's Carnival. Through the eyes of the Philadelphians, Gary was invisible, a hero, or a potential villain. For the passersby, there was no inconspicuous fellow city dweller. There was only the irrelevant, the personally familiar and the alien, and justifiably so. Within the first ten minutes of entering the city, Gary stumbled upon several citizens gathered around yet another corpse.

Gary approached the throng. "What happened?"

A young woman turned to answer. "Another murder. Heard it's the eighth tonight."

"I'm trying to find an officer," Gary said, "to report a murder at the Carnival."

"That's nine now!" another man said. "Nine murders in one night! Why isn't there an investigation underway? Where are the police?"

"I don't know," Gary said. "Let me see if I can find one."

Gary traipsed deeper into the heart of the city, sacrificing the bird's eye view from Uncle Sam's Carnival for the pseudo-intimate mole's eye view, until he stumbled upon a robust, pasty-faced man drinking on the brick outcrop of an apartment building wall.

"What're you doing?" the man asked.

"I'm looking for an officer," Gary replied.

"You've found one." The man unscrewed the cap from a pint-sized bottle and drank deeply. "But he's off duty."

"There's been a murder, several actually," Gary announced.

"Sure, there have been many," the man observed, taking another drink.

"At the carnival, someone's been killed. And on the way here I saw another body."

"It's not uncommon in the cities," the man replied. "And I'm not going to lie. If they're not caught in the act, it's damn near impossible to locate culprits." He screwed the cap tight on his bottle, but loosened it and took a third drink. "We've a few poor folks down at the precinct for drunken and disorderly. You can rough one up, if it'll make you feel any better."

"I'd rather sleep knowing I won't be the next victim," Gary said.

"Then I'll beat a confession out of one of them."

"What about the real killer?"

"What is a real criminal in this day and age?"

"One who commits a crime."

"You see anyone do it?"

Gary shook his head. "My girlfriend was the first on the scene, but she's blind."

"Aye," the man said. "Aren't we all out here?" Pause. "Tell you what. Why don't you look out for that girlfriend of yours, and call me if you see anything suspicious?"

"What if the killer strikes again?"

"Try to get a look at him next time."

"Isn't that your job?"

"You're out of my jurisdiction. You'd be better off telling the papers. Fear'll get the ball rolling on this one. Don't tell them I sent you, though."

"Thanks," Gary said, "I think. But where do I find the papers?"

The man whistled. "Murder!" he shouted.

Suddenly, out of the darkness emerged several apparitions that encompassed Gary and the man. Gary thought he heard the sound of hissing, but, upon closer scrutiny, found it was only the sound of graphite on paper, interspersed with a chorus of whispered inquiries. "Another murder?" They seemed more fascinated than appalled. "Where was the murder? The murder?" they asked.

"The carnival," Gary replied.

"Uncle Sam'sssss?" They asked in unison. "Uncle Sam's Carnival?" Their voices assumed a rhetorical tone. "The Carnival," they said. "They're there. We're there." And then the figures withdrew again into the darkness.

"I guess I should follow them," Gary said.

"Oh no," the officer replied. "Like they said, they're already there. Always a minute late to a crime. Always right on time for a report."

"How do I get back?" Gary asked.

"Follow the wealth. There's always filth and sadness at the heart of every city. Walk away from here, away from poverty until you reach the city limits. From there you shouldn't have a problem."

"What if I get lost on the outskirts?"

"Follow hope."

"Hope?" Gary glanced upward, beckoning a reply with his gaze, but the officer had passed out. Perturbed by the cryptic, drunken ramblings, Gary walked down the cleanest street whenever he came to a crossroads until he found the outer limits. But it was then that he became disoriented, for there was no sign of hope. Continuing his search, a shrill cry distracted him. He followed the source until it became a brisk shout, emanating from a young boy.

"Morning edition!" he shouted. "Gary: the near-invisible man brightens cityscape at Uncle Sam's Carnival of Copulating Inanimals! A star is born!"

Gary approached the boy and requested a copy. On the

front page, he saw an ink rendering of himself bowing before a plethora of black dots, presumably the heads of onlookers at the carnival. The headline read exactly as the boy had announced.

Gary thumbed a hole in his abdomen and extracted a slimy nickel. The boy shook his head. "On the house, buddy. They're replacing the headline in an hour, anyway. Early edition's already obsolete."

Gary's ego momentarily lapsed. "Why?" he asked.

"200 people dead and counting," the boy explained. "The terrible sells better than the terrific. Can't say why. Puts everybody in a solemn mood." He stopped then, studied Gary's face. "Hey, ain't you? You are! You're Gary! I heard you were coming to town!"

"Do you know which way the carnival is?" Gary asked the boy.

"Follow your flyers," he said. "A pleasure to meet you, by the way."

"You too," Gary said, following the trail of encouraging flyers back to the carnival, each bolstering his ego in increments along the way.

* * *

Upon returning, Gary was met by Liberty, and several of the media apparitions. They scurried quickly from person to person, taking notes on the body's position, whispering in unison, "What did you ssseeee?"

"Just the facts?" another set of them asked.

"Just the facts," the remaining echoed in their snake-like tone.

Liberty was the first to notice Gary as he approached the scene. "Gary!" She ran to meet him. "Are you ok?"

"I'm fine."

"Did you get a hold of the police?"

He shook his head dismissively. "Yes. But they don't seem too concerned."

"What do you mean?"

"The man I spoke to was drunk," Gary explained. "And pretty much implied that, were he sober, he still wouldn't care."

"That's terrible," Liberty replied.

"Maybe he was just overwhelmed. A newspaper boy on the edge of the city said there have been 200 murders tonight alone."

"Actually," the media apparitions whispered, "the count has nearly doubled now."

"When did they get here?" Gary asked.

"They came almost as soon as you left. It was the strangest thing. They even got here before Uncle Sam."

"Where was he?" Gary asked.

"He said he was resting, and then he left to meet an officer about the murder."

Gary paused. "I went to his tent, but he wasn't there."

Liberty placed her hand in Gary's. "Do you think he had something to do with this?"

He pulled away. "No. No, that's not possible." He surveyed the scene. "Have you talked to the press?"

"Yes," she said. "I've told them all I know. They want to talk to you."

"We already talked to the boy," the press replied. "But we didn't get everything we needed."

"Ask anything you want," Gary said, confident, although the press had apparently been eavesdropping on his conversation with Liberty, encompassing them without their knowledge.

"What was the first thing you sssaw?" they asked.

"I saw the young woman on the ground, a small puddle of blood at her waist."

"The woman," they replied. "*The* woman. Not *a* woman?"

44

"The woman who was murdered."

"It...soundsssss as if you knew her."

"I've never seen the girl before in my life," Gary said.

"I've never smelled her on him," Liberty added.

The apparitions scribbled in their notepads.

Just then, Uncle Sam hobbled slowly forward alongside the pasty, drunken officer Gary had met in the heart of the city. The press broke its circle, allowing them in.

"Uncle Sam, are you ok?" Gary asked.

"I'm fine," Sam said. "What's going on here?"

"Just the facts," the press replied. "Questions."

The officer puffed his chest. "Incidentally, that's what I'm here for, too."

Gary broke in. "I thought the case didn't matter to you."

The officer waved a paper before him, handing it off to Gary. "Didn't you see the headlines? Fresh off the press: 'Mass Murder Hits Philadelphia, Authorities Mystified.' It's a matter of reputation now. We simply have to find out who did this." The officer glared at Liberty. "Was it you? You appear quite suspicious with those black holes in your head, deary. Not the average-looking sort, are you?"

Instinctively, Gary pushed Liberty behind him. "She didn't do anything!"

Sam turned to address the officer. "I told you before. You can ask all the questions you want, but don't implicate my employees. These two were not present when the girl was murdered."

"How do you know?" the press asked, their hands scratching at paper like the needle of a lie detector test.

"Yeah," the officer added. "How do you know?"

Uncle Sam cast a glance in Gary and Liberty's direction, one that suggested the importance of the partial fabrication about to leave his lips. "They were with me," he said. "Almost the entire evening."

"That's not what sssshe said," the press whispered.

Uncle Sam looked down. "She did not know I was there."

Liberty turned to Gary. A tear gathered at the cusp of her empty sockets. "Is this true, Gary?"

Gary nodded, looked back at Uncle Sam. "It is," he said, though he had no knowledge of Sam's presence earlier that evening, nor whether Sam was lying or telling the truth.

"Uncle, why would you invade our privacy?"

"It's not that, Liberty. It's just, I needed something new...straight to video, you know? I—it's not as if you did anything."

"What did you think we were going to do?" Liberty asked. "You perverts!" She slapped Gary's lower jaw with such severity that it was difficult for her to dislodge her hand. Gary assisted in her endeavor. "Thank you," she said, wiping the tears from her empty sockets. "Goodbye."

"Liberty, don't leave!" Gary pleaded.

She turned away without a reply.

"We've all we need," the press said. Once more, they began to recede into the shadows.

"Were you really watching us?" Gary asked.

Sam nodded.

"How could you?"

"I'm sorry. The carnival isn't doing as well as I'd initially hoped. I know you've brought many in, but it's the carnival games we're losing money on. And without Ignatius behind the camera, the video releases have been flopping. I needed another with you, Gary."

"You could have just asked me. We could have found a way to make something work. I could have filmed the inanimals for you."

"No. I wanted you and Liberty. Acting on command isn't enough. The audience, they can tell when your heart's not in it. But when I saw you tonight with my niece after the show, I knew you were interested in her. Do you know how hard it is to translate such passion to the screen? Only you—"

"I've heard enough!" Gary turned for his tent.

"Gary!"

"I don't want to hear it!" he shouted.

"You!" The officer called. "Wait just a minute!"

Gary stopped, his back still turned to the officer and Sam.

"I want to make this clear to both of you. You're not to leave the premises tonight. I'll be back for further questioning in the morning."

Gary absorbed the request and resumed walking.

* * *

When Gary returned to his tent, he found Liberty waiting there for him.

"Liberty, I—I didn't know he was there, either. I was just covering for him."

"Sure," she sobbed.

"I'm serious. Please believe me. I would never do anything to hurt you." Again, he wiped away her tears. "I don't want to see you cry."

She looked up at him, and though she was blind, Gary felt the piercing emptiness of her eyes.

"Liberty, your eyes..." He corrected himself. "Those black holes," he said. "Sometimes when I look into them, I feel like I'm being drawn in like..." he shuffled through his memory bank for an appropriate simile, but was ultimately short changed, "well, like black holes."

Liberty laughed through her tears. "Oh Gary, you have no skill with words."

Gary parted the curtain to the tent's entrance. "Come on," he said, guiding her past the threshold. "Stay with me tonight."

"Why? So you can film us for Uncle Sam?"

"I won't try anything. We'll just sleep. That's all."

"If you try anything, I'm leaving."

"I won't lay a finger on you. I promise."
She nodded and followed him to bed.

* * *

In a nearby cart, Uncle Sam and Bob worked diligently through the night on Sam's most recent endeavor. Carefully, Bob extracted a dropper and let several drops of Regenagent #32 mingle with a small sample of blood. Nearby, Sam prepared a microscope.

"Damn it, Bob! Why didn't you clean the bodies up like I told you?"

"I tried, sir."

"You tried?" Sam said, steadying himself momentarily to place the Regenagent-laced blood on a glass slide. "Every body was found! Couldn't you have at least made an attempt to cover them?"

"500 bodies is a lot to account for, sir. There are too many of your shadows to clean up after."

"500? Christ! I'd hoped for a dozen bodies between here and the far end of Philadelphia. Have you done a headcount on the inanimals yet?"

"Not yet, sir."

"I'd like that done as soon as possible. We need to know the Regenagent's reach. For all we know, it could be drawing souls into our inanimate objects from all over the country."

"Yes, sir," Bob said.

Sam placed the slide under the microscope. He squinted, brought his eye to the lens. "Nothing. Did you mix the sample with Regenagent like I asked?"

"Yes. It's not working?"

"It's not doing shit." He pulled away from the microscope. "Why did you think this was going to work again?"

"Gary, sir. You found him in the scrap room, right next to the dead body." Pause. "I think he's a byproduct of Regenagent #32."

"He's a blob of mucous in the shape of a person."

"He *is* a person. He thinks. He acts. He speaks. He's not like the other inanimals."

"I know he's special. That's why I was grooming him for my position."

Bob looked up, hopefully. "Have you changed your mind about retiring, sir?"

"No." Uncle Sam returned his eye to the microscope. "Still nothing. I wish we had one of the bodies, Bob."

"There'll be more, sir. In the next town."

Sam took the dropper of Regenagent. "There better be. We need to figure out something fast." He let drops trickle onto the ground near his feet. A few slivers of shadow broke away and hissed as they left the cart. "These shadows insist on performing behind the scenes. Gary isn't securing the public interest like I had hoped he would. I need something new. A boy of blood, a goat made of piss, anything to secure interest."

"We could use my shadow, sir," Bob suggested. "Or my blood."

Sam, suddenly a shade paler, turned to face him. "It won't work. You're human."

Bob was taken aback. "Sir, you look ill. Are you ok?"

"I'm fine." Sam walked to a mirror in the corner, noted lines carving their way into his face, into his very being. He smiled. "I'll be damned."

"Sir?"

Sam took Bob by the shoulders. "This is wonderful, Bob!"

"What is, sir?"

"Look at me!" He held Bob close. "I'm sickly! I'm losing power!" He turned again towards the mirror. "Bob, tell the media apparitions I want a mass murder story above the fold in every city across America tomorrow morning! I want a body on every corner in every city!"

"But why?"

"You heard the detective. Philly's in a panic over the recent murders. People are preoccupied with survival on the streets. They're not in the least bit concerned with the American dream."

"You want them to forget about you, sir?"

"I told you before. I'm too fucking old for this."

The wind began to pick up. Bob walked to the curtain, opened it to the elements outside. "Storm's coming."

"Pack the tents. We should leave."

"What about the HAARP?"

"It's already running. Doesn't seem to be doing much against this front." Sam gripped his hat to prevent it from blowing away. "We better move fast. I want to get out of here before the storm catches up with us."

* * *

Later that evening, Gary awoke from a deep slumber as he lay with Liberty. He rose from bed to check on the inanimals and found the caravan in motion, along with the entire carnival. Uncle Sam, Bob and the others had apparently packed up and set for the next city against the officer's wishes. Gary looked to the horizon and suddenly understood why. In the distance, something ebbed and flowed through the night. Though the evening was black, something deeper than black—or not black but simply nothingness—swelled. It appeared as if the entire world was being wiped clean with a magic roll of toilet paper. He contemplated waking Liberty, but upon seeing her sleep so peacefully, found his place again at her side and let sleep overcome him, too.

Chapter 5: Liberty Lost

The next morning, Akimbo's insistent banging at the cart's edge awoke Gary. The convoy had apparently stopped, and the pets, being the first to sense this, found their way outside to graze in the fields. Gary crawled from the bed as gently as possible so as not to wake Liberty. He walked to the curtain, opened it quietly. "What is it, boy?" he whispered.

Akimbo edged away from the tent, beckoning Gary by tapping his forelegs upon the ground. Gary noted Liberty, still sleeping peacefully, and followed Akimbo to the other inanimals.

"You want me to start my chores?" Gary asked. "It's barely daylight."

Akimbo stamped his forelegs into the ground playfully.

"Alright, alright. I think you're just eager to play with your friends, aren't you?" Gary walked to the desk cage and removed the tarp. "Whoa!"

Akimbo quaked with fear, for what awaited them under the tarp was not a cage of happy-go-lucky desks of playful disposition, but an overstuffed prison, broken legs and wood chips protruding from behind the bars. The heap moved, implying some of the desks were still alive. Gary opened the cage quickly, releasing a pile of the dead, followed by many injured and half-alive desks. They writhed on the ground.

Gary pointed towards the front of the convoy, directing Akimbo. "Find Sam!" he shouted, not just for the sake of the injured desks, but for Akimbo's well-being. To see so many of his kind in such shape was likely detrimental. For though Uncle Sam had told him the inanimals could not feel, Gary's taser told him otherwise.

Akimbo scurried away to find Sam while Gary tended to the injured and covered the dead with a tarp.

By the time Akimbo retrieved Sam, Gary had separated the dead and concealed them, which was his goal.

Sam staggered behind the anxious desk. "What's happened here?" he asked.

Gary noticed the lines on Sam's pallid face had grown deeper. He appeared nothing if not sick. "Are you ok?"

"Don't worry about me. What's so pressing that you had your mutt drag me from sleep?"

Gary pointed to the tarp-covered carnage on the ground. "There were more again. Hundreds this time. The desks, they're breeding or something," he explained. "Didn't Bob tell you?"

"That's...terrible."

"There were just a few at first. But now there are so many they're suffocating, shattering under the pressure."

Sam limped forward and looked under the tarp. "How many did you say there were?"

"I lost count around 100, but there are parts for several others."

"How many are still alive?"

"About twenty," Gary estimated.

"As long as we have enough for the show."

"They're dying in there!" Gary shouted. "Do you have any explanation for why this is happening?"

Uncle Sam dropped the edge of the canvas and turned to Gary. "It's none of your concern. I hired you to make the inanimals fuck, not to ask questions."

"I also take care of the inanimals! I think I need to know so I can help make this as easy on us and them as possible!"

"You want to make it easy? Scrap the metal. Use the wood for fire. All of the inanimals end up being consumed anyway. In case you haven't noticed, the only ones that last longer than a few weeks are the pets, and that's because we choose to let them live so long."

Gary didn't keep track of the inanimals on an individual

basis. It had never occurred to him that the ones used in film and in the carnival might not be the same ones he met upon arrival.

"What's wrong, Gary? Do you feel sorry for them?" Sam approached one of the wounded inanimals, stroked its polished cherry top. "They're not humans," he explained. "Christ, they're not even fucking animals!" He took the injured desk by the front leg and pulled at a rear leg with his other hand, splitting it in half. The desk convulsed until the life left it. "They're inanimals, Gary. We made them for our entertainment."

As their argument continued, the wind began to pick up.

"But they're alive!" Gary shouted.

"No, Gary. They're cogs. Walking, performing cogs."

"You made them that way!"

Uncle Sam's hat began to lift in the wind. He caught it with both hands. "They did it to themselves."

In the distance, Bob and his crew were struggling with one of the tents. Gary and Sam, attracted to the scene by a loud crash, turned to see the tent collapse before being erected fully.

Sam clasped his hat and nodded in Bob's direction. "Come on."

Bob ran to meet them. "Get your first aid kit, Sam. One of the workers, he's injured. Tent pole fell on him."

Sam glanced out of the corner of his eye, noting the approaching storm on the horizon. "Gary, get the desks—the healthy ones—back in their cages."

"What about the injured?"

"Leave them."

As Gary ran back to the cages, Sam turned to Bob. "Did you contact the media?"

"Yes, sir. A murder on every corner in every city, story above the fold, just as you asked. The shadows will be finishing up on the west coast this evening. The reactions reported by the apparitions are similar to those in Philadelphia."

"Ok. The Regenagent isn't quite as powerful as we thought. Only about 100 of those murdered last night ended up in the cart today."

"That's probably a good thing, sir. Otherwise, we'd have thousands and thousands of inanimals to account for."

"You have a point." Sam drew his hand across his face. The scaly, withered texture reminded him of eating dried apricots with his sister when they were children. He smiled. "Get your men. We should be moving on."

"Yes, sir."

* * *

Once at the cages, Gary called to his pet. "Akimbo, wake Liberty for me. I need her help."

Akimbo scampered off. Liberty returned with him only a few minutes later, still wiping the sleep from her empty sockets. "What's wrong, Gary?" she asked.

"I need you to help the uninjured into their cage. I'm taking some of the injured to my tent."

Akimbo cringed at the spread of injured desks, and, thanks to the heavy winds, the uncovered plethora of desks broken beyond repair.

"What happened?" Liberty asked.

"I don't know. There're more every time we reach a new city. Got any ideas?"

She shook her head.

"Alright, help the flock. I'm going to take as many of the injured as I can with us."

Gary carried two desks at a time, one in each hand by the front legs, and managed to pack four into his tent before the storm was upon the caravan. Again, it was the rolling nothingness, engulfing everything before it, leaving only a swirling current not unlike oil mixed with water. It reminded

Gary of the day Uncle Sam guided him to the carnival for the first time, that gaseous fissure between his world and the open range. In the distance, Gary could see people from the city running from the storm. He found Liberty at his side then, prompting his attention with urgency. "There's more!" she cried. "The desks! They're doubling! Splitting like cells! I can smell them all around me!"

Gary remained fixed upon the storm. "That's impossible."

"I've already closed the cage, but they're dying in there! I don't know what to do!"

"You have to get in the tent," Gary insisted.

She did not hear him. For the first time since childhood, Liberty found that she could see. She couldn't discern what lay immediately before her, but in the distance, where Gary saw nothingness, Liberty saw clearly. She watched as the smoke-like current encompassed the citizens inhabiting the town on the horizon, their screams cut short as they evaporated.

The storm advanced quickly. Mesmerized, Liberty walked towards it. It reminded her of childhood, of heat exuding from the pavement of a trailer park she grew up in as she played hopscotch with friends.

"Liberty!" Gary cried. But she could not hear him over the wind. She breached the nothingness. Gary turned for Uncle Sam's tent, running against the pace of the storm with Akimbo in stride. He opened the tent, and therein found Uncle Sam, his face now riddled with pockmarks, dousing desks and chairs with a small vial of Regenagent #32.

"Liberty!" he cried. "She's trapped in the storm! We have to save her!"

Uncle Sam poured the remainder of the vial on a large black futon. "This is the only way, Gary."

He tugged at Sam's vest. "We must!"

Sam broke his grasp. "Damn it, Gary! I said this is the only way! It's too late, don't you see? She's gone! The only way to save her now is to imbue the furniture with her soul."

"What are you talking about?"

"You think their souls come out of thin air?" Uncle Sam rubbed the Regenagent into each piece of furniture dutifully. "Those people dying out there in the storm. We're giving them a second chance."

"You're turning them into furniture!?" Gary fled the safety of the tent for the brunt of the storm. "Liberty!" he cried again, and before he could think twice, he too was enmeshed in the nothingness, rendered as blind as his love.

Bob started for him.

"Leave him!" Uncle Sam insisted. "He's worthless to us now."

"He's the star of the show," Bob said.

"We can always find another."

"He's our friend."

Uncle Sam continued caressing the furniture imbued with Reagent #32.

* * *

Gary walked slowly now, his speed dictated by the current. With hands outstretched, he cried for Liberty and groped the air as if with every movement he might find her. Eventually the winds grew too heavy, and he fell to his knees. His cries turned to inane mutterings, his crawl to baby steps. He trudged onward, calling to Liberty until he felt strong arms around him. A familiar voice echoed in his ear. "Let go, Gary," it said.

"Ignatius?" Gary asked. "Mr. Wakefield? I know your voice... Who are you?"

The voice answered. "Liberty's fine, Gary. Just let go."

Chapter 6: Liberty Found

Gary awoke, afraid to open his eyes. The wind had ceased; the only indication of time and space he had was an overwhelming sense of warmth dancing on his eyelids. He remained in a fetal position until a voice beckoned him. "Don't be afraid, Gary. You're safe."

"Am I alive?" Gary asked as he opened his eyes. Before him a portly, middle-aged man garbed in white stood, arms outstretched.

"You are alive. Now come. Walk with me."

He tried to get up, but to his surprise found himself already walking. "What just happened?"

"You willed yourself to action," the man said.

"Where are we?"

"We're in the realm of global consciousness," the man replied, anticipating the next question. "I am Buddha-Christ."

"Buddha-Christ?"

"Yes, those two and many more. But, to keep things simple, we'll stick with that."

"Are you Christ from the Bible?" Gary asked.

"Well, I'm a combination of that Christ and the real Christ." He looked at Gary, perhaps deliberating whether or not he was worth imparting the details of his existence to. "I'm a combination of all central Gods in the myths of all nations, all individuals. Since you are familiar with Buddha and Christ, I manifest as a mix of the two. Were you from another tribe, say, the Yanomamo from Brazil, I would manifest as yet another God."

"So, this is heaven?" Gary asked.

"No. And it isn't hell, either."

"Why am I here?"

"Because you're special, Gary."

Oddly enough, Gary, at a moment other than the present, might have agreed. But in the presence of this great figure, Gary felt insignificant and very small.

Buddha-Christ continued, "There are two kinds of people who change the world, Gary. There are people who change it with action and people who do so with thought. You fall into the latter of these two categories." Buddha-Christ walked to a nearby tree and plucked a strange, flowering fruit resembling the female genitalia from it. "Would you like one?" he asked.

Gary nodded reluctantly, but, when he partook, it tasted incredibly sweet and sent orgasmic shivers down his vitreous humor spine. As they pressed onward, Gary tried hard to pay attention to the Buddha-Christ, but there were so many sights around him, which were only apparent out of the corner of his eye. Upon looking directly at anything, it would immediately disappear, like stars in the night sky sometimes do. It took all of his concentration not to look at what he was not fully looking at in the first place.

The Buddha-Christ continued, "Of those who influence the world with thought, there are yet more categories. There are those who influence the world via a sort of democratic system, and those who just outright imbue the global collective with their imagination, thereby turning their dreams into reality. The first of these, those who influence through democracy, must convince others of their beliefs in order to change reality. The latter simply override the democratic function, thereby creating an extremely powerful, yet extremely volatile, circumstance."

"Which category do I fall into?" Gary asked. "Regardless, I mean the world no harm."

"Christopher Columbus felt the same way in 1492," Buddha-Christ replied. "Did you know that the earth was once indeed flat?"

Gary laughed. "That's preposterous."

"Well, I suppose that reply is better than some. Had you replied that the earth is still flat, it might actually have become so."

"You're telling me I have the power to change reality?"

"Yes."

"Did I think the carnival and Uncle Sam into existence?"

"Don't be so conceited. I said you can change reality, not that you created it."

Gary was relieved at this reply. The thought of being the only independent conscious mind in the carnival frightened him. To be truly alone, he realized, was the worst thing imaginable. Gary closed his eyes and tried to 'think' himself back to the carnival.

"Not yet, Gary," Buddha-Christ said. "There is more. Below the global realm of consciousness there is the national or cultural realm. Below that there is the sub-cultural realm, and, of course, finally, the realm of the individuals. You can't simply think yourself back home from here. You will have to find what you came here looking for."

"I don't know why I'm here," Gary reflected. He thought hard, remembered Akimbo pulling at his ankle, the heavy winds. The nothingness encompassing him, nothingness like those deep, black sockets in... "Liberty," he recalled.

"Liberty," Buddha-Christ mused. "Keep your eyes peeled on your journey."

"How do I get from one point to the next?" Gary asked.

"Well, that's where it gets complicated. You have to close your eyes as you walk, which is going to interfere with my last suggestion to keep your eyes open. You'll figure it out."

He did as the Buddha-Christ suggested, and found himself in the same surroundings. "It's not working," he said, glancing at his right side where Buddha-Christ had accompanied him. He was no longer there. "Buddha-Christ?" Gary looked from side to side. There was no response. He was alone. Again, he closed his eyes and walked onward until he heard the sound of rockets blazing and felt flecks of hot shrapnel raining down upon his back. "Get off the field, you fuckin' wanker!" a young man shouted, pulling Gary into a nearby trench.

Gary was surrounded by what appeared to be leprechauns in New York Yankee outfits.

"Christ! E's made of spit!" one of the leprechauns shouted.

"Whose bright idea was it to bring 'im in 'ere?" said another.

"What's going on?" Gary asked.

"Someone dragged a gelatin man into our trenches! Prolly sent by the British!"

"'E ain't British," another replied. "E's an American just like half of us are."

Gary looked around. "What realm is this?"

"Realm? I'll be goddamned if I know what realm it is, but this 'ere's the American-Irish revolution against the oppression of Mother Britain."

"Mother me arse!" Another voice shot back. "She's a hooer, that's what she is!"

"Listen, grease man," the nearest leprechaun said, handing Gary a rifle. "We ain't got much time for explainin'. You here to fight or to fuck off?"

Gary took the rifle. "Guess I'm going to fight."

"Good," the leprechaun said. "We're goin' over the edge in five."

"Whose soil are we on?" Gary asked.

"Half Dublin, half New York, the best we can tell. Bomb!"

The men crouched in their trench as several mortars passed.

The Yankee leprechaun continued, "Y'ever have a dream where two towns ya visited in the waking world are connected geographically, all bunched-like in one area?"

Gary shook his head.

"Neither have I, but that's basically what's goin' on 'ere." A loud horn blew in the distance. "That's the signal."

The leprechaun butted out a large cigar that moments before dangled from his lips. "You fuckin' ready?"

To this inquiry, Gary nodded.

"Let's get the bastards!"

Reluctantly, Gary topped the trenches with the leprechauns. They crawled forward, flat on their bellies, the fire from machine gun nests hovering above serving as incentive. Each movement the leprechauns made, Gary followed suit. When they rose to cover ground, he rose to cover ground. When enough leprechauns dropped around him, some from incoming fire, some from common sense, Gary did likewise. Twice he found himself riddled with fire, the hot lead searing his gelatin body, burning through his gelatin lungs. But Gary continued to breathe.

"Grease boy's invincible!" one of the leprechauns shouted.

"Aye," another replied. "I'd give me left nut to be made of that goo right now!"

"One thing's for sure," another said. "Keep movin' or at best you'll be hamburger!"

In a span of only minutes, half of Gary's Yankee leprechaun platoon had been mowed down. Yet the survivors trudged onwards, Gary following closely, occasionally rising to fire at the opposition.

"Christ!" one of the leprechauns shouted. "We've got no feckin' chance! Where's the commander?!"

"'E's Dead!"

"What about private Donahue?"

"E's dead too!"

"Who's next in command?"

"Private O'Donnell!"

"Where's he?"

"He got shot as we were coming outta the trenches!"

"Well, who the fuck's in charge, then?"

"Nobody's willin' to take that position," one offered. "All the heads keep getting shot."

"Can we all agree to retreat, then?"

"Wait a minute!" one of the Yankee-leprechauns shouted. "We can't give up yet! We still got goo boy, right?"

They all nodded in unison between the strobe-light effect created by flashing mortar.

"Then let's get the sonsabitches! Charge!"

Gary rose with the men. He felt the bullets bear down upon him as he closed his eyes. As they neared the opposition, the atmosphere fell silent. Gary assumed he was dead, waited for that source of light once more, but heard only the call of birds as he ran headlong into one of the largest trees he'd ever seen. It was then that Gary decided to abandon his rifle and, without questioning his transition from war to peaceful forest, moved onward.

* * *

For two days and two nights, Gary walked through the forest. The trees were as tall as they were dense, nearly blocking out daylight entirely, leaving a parched landscape below with little foliage. After the speckled forest top went from appearing star-riddled to black a second time, Gary heard the sound of echoing cries. After following the cries for a considerable amount of time, he saw a small fire burning in the distance.

On the third morning, Gary finally arrived at the source of the now dwindling fire, and found there a blue ox four stories tall, and a man twice as large, curled in a fetal position and sobbing to himself.

"What's wrong, good sir?" Gary asked.

"What?" the large man asked. "Who's there?"

"My name is Gary, and I'm on a quest to find my girl-friend, Liberty."

"Well, you probably think you're on the right track," the man replied. "This being the forest of freedom and all."

"And you are?"

"Paul Bunyan," the man said, offering his hand.

Gary reached out and smeared his greasy palm on the giant's pinky finger. "Pleased to meet you," he said.

"Well, there's not really much to be pleased about."

"I don't mean to be contrary," Gary explained, "but, after the war, I find this a rather pleasant alternative."

"Well, it just hasn't set in for you yet, then," Bunyan said.

"What's that?"

"Look at us. We're surrounded by so many trees, can't see a damned thing outside a thirty-foot radius. The fire's so far from my face; when I stand it looks like a speck on the ground."

"Can't you just cut down the trees?"

"I've lost my axe."

Gary observed Bunyan's ox gnawing at the handle. "It's right over there," he said.

"Look," Bunyan replied, tears welling in his eyes once more. "I just don't fucking feel like it, okay! I'm depressed. I'm lonely, and I feel the whole thing was a sham, coming out west. They said, 'Oh, there'll be a city of gold, and acres of land to settle and'...and a bunch of goddamned blood-soaked soils. People dying from disease. It's a goddamned mess."

"But in my time the west is settled. Though there's danger, there's also opportunity. And the tales of gold are true."

"And what does gold get you?" Bunyan asked. "It starts off as wealth. Then it's greed, corruption. Gold's the root of evil. That's why I went on strike. I'm not chopping down another damned tree from this point onward."

Suddenly, the ox stopped gnawing at the base of Bunyan's axe handle and whispered into Gary's ear. "Pay no attention to him," it said. "He's a victim of the very system he perpetuates. A little introspection would serve him well, but he can't get past feeling sorry for himself." The ox returned to chewing on the axe handle.

"Introspection?" Gary asked.

"He needs to look inside himself." The ox said. "*Inside.* You're not the brightest fellow, are you?"

Gary reached into the area where his heart should have been, digging through the objects he had collected. When he reached the small of his back, he sensed a small light. He grasped this light and pulled it forward until it was at the cusp of his vitreous humor ribs. The light became a hand, which he continued to pull. Then the hand became an arm, and a shoulder. Then he saw the deep sockets he had come to know and love. He felt the coughs of a vitreous humor-smothered Liberty reverberate in his chest. He continued to pull until she was upon him. "Liberty!" he cried, holding her at arm's length. "I have something to tell you…" He pulled her close. "I love you."

Gary closed his eyes and savored the moment. The last thing he remembered was the modest sniffle of Bunyan's ox. Then a cool wind against his face told him he was no longer in the forest of freedom. He opened his eyes and found himself once again alone on the open range before several carts, upturned and scattered about the landscape.

He returned to his cart and, with the help of a few desks, turned it upright. The desks pleaded with him to release the others, but Gary was too distraught to be of any service. He wept for what he now thought was a dream, for the illusion of redemption promised to him by the Buddha-Christ. He wept for Liberty, who, thanks to the transport of dream, he had now lost twice.

When he finally mustered enough strength to leave his cart, he was greeted by a small futon, black and tattered. The futon, like the desks, was insistent, demanded that Gary help the others from their cages. "Leave me alone," he whimpered, going from caravan to caravan, looking for Uncle Sam, Bob, or any other who might be able to explain what had happened.

The futon etched in the sand. Plumes of dust obscured its message. Finally, when they settled and Gary turned to the futon's scrawls, he saw legible words. "Gone," the ground read.

"Uncle Sam is gone?" Gary asked rhetorically. "No shit."

The futon banged emphatically.

"Then I must find Liberty," he replied. Closing his lids, he thought of his lover, the black sockets that swallowed his soul the first time he laid eyes upon her. He walked for nearly a mile, and then opened his eyes. Again, he was met only with the futon.

At this, he swatted the furniture vehemently. "Away!" he shouted. "Shoo!"

Stubbornly, the futon scrawled again in the sand.

"On with it!" Gary exclaimed as the futon brushed and rubbed the ground in large circles, resulting in the following message: "It's me, Gary."

"Liberty?" he asked plaintively, then, "It can't be true."

Suddenly, the futon rushed him from behind, knocking his legs from underneath him. He found himself on the outstretched futon, struggling to escape. It cradled him with a gentle touched paralleled only by Liberty's the night she helped repair his arm.

"No," he whispered to himself. "This is some trick."

Then Gary remembered Uncle Sam dousing the futon in Regenagent #32. He started to cry. "I thought I had lost you again, Liberty." He turned and hugged Liberty-futon with all of his strength. "We'll turn you back somehow. That I promise."

Liberty-futon felt Gary's viscous member throb between her cushions. She resisted, but as he kissed her armrests, she melted and allowed him to penetrate her cotton-polyester labia.

Between Gary's gentle thrusts, Liberty heard the echo of something distant in her mind. The sound grew in intensity until the unintelligible became a coherent string of words: *I love you.*

"Did you say something?" Liberty asked, but no audible words issued forth, for she no longer had a mouth.

Gary paused. "What?" he asked.

You—you heard me? she thought.

"You asked if I said something." He smiled. "I didn't, but I was thinking—" He stopped speaking, thought instead— *that I love you.*

Gary couldn't see Liberty's expression, but he could feel it. In his mind, he saw her as she was when they first met: wide-socketed and smiling modestly.

"I love you too, Gary," she thought-spoke.

And it was there on the open range that Gary and Liberty's son, Self-Glorified Hedonism, was conceived. But that is a tale for another time, another place.

Chapter 7: Showdown

After an illustrious night of lovemaking, Gary and Liberty gathered the inanimals from their cages and proceeded with a count before determining what they would do next. They found that they had nearly 400 desks, half of which were injured. In another cage, they found several bureaus, three of which were operational. There were also two caravans, six futons and eighty couches.

As all gathered before Gary, who stood atop one of the two caravans remaining, the situation did not look promising.

"From what I understand," Gary began, "most of you were, at one point, hard working civilians in one of the east coast cities visited by Uncle Sam. I can't say I have the answers you're looking for. Nor can I promise to find those answers. But I'd like to try."

The crowd roared as desks swayed from side to side, banging against one another in applause.

"There aren't enough inanimals to face Sam," Liberty warned. "He's likely accumulated a greater force."

"I'm not looking for retribution. I just want answers." Gary turned to address the inanimals once more. "Some of you came to this land for 'opportunity.' Well, not all is lost. At least we've found strength again through a common goal." He paced to and fro. "While none of us know how far we'll have to travel to find Uncle Sam, nor if we'll make it through the brunt of the storm, nor what he'll have in store for us when we get there, find him we must!"

The crowd broke into applause again, only to be hushed by Gary's calm gestures.

"We don't know his exact whereabouts," he explained. "But I think pursuing the storm is the best chance we've got. I'd say the storm's presence in the distance is indication enough that Sam hasn't gone far. It follows that HAARP like clockwork."

The audience roared, the sound of metal on metal and wood on metal echoing across the plains. The small group of inanimals then mobilized. Gary and Liberty led them.

* * *

Just beyond the storm, Uncle Sam, Bob and the media apparitions urged the remnants of their convoy, led by two hulking Ferris wheels, toward their new destination.

Uncle Sam looked into a mirror. His ears had begun to wither and crack. His nose was all but gone. "Damn it!" he shouted. "Why am I not dead yet?"

The curtain to Sam's cart opened. "Why did we turn back?" Bob asked.

"We can't outrun this storm all the way to the west coast. Our HAARP is losing power, and, when it dies out, that storm will overtake us. We have to get back to the factory." Sam wiped puss from erupting boils on his face and pointed to the billowing smoke stacks on the coastline. "We've not much farther to go."

"Don't you think you should see a doctor, sir? I've been watching you for some time now. I think you have the AIDS or something."

"It's too late for doctors," Sam said, catching the discharge on his face with his shirtsleeve. "I just want to get back home, so I can die in peace."

"I thought you were immortal, sir."

"I think I've finally found a way around that." Sam poked his head outside. "We better get back to the reigns."

"I can take them for you," Bob offered, "but they're more than capable on their own."

"Sure, but they're slow as hell unless you're at them. I'd like to see us home as quickly as possible."

Sam took his seat behind the large Ferris wheels. Bob sat next to him at the front edge of the cart. He dragged his feet in the sand and watched his toes etch a snake-like trail as the convoy pushed forward. "Ever since we started this journey, the storm has been gaining on us. But it seems to stop when we stop. It never hits us."

Uncle Sam lowered the reigns. "And?"

"Could the HAARP be causing the storm?" Bob asked.

"The HAARP protects us," Uncle Sam assured him.

"Yes, but at what cost?"

Uncle Sam opened the door to the cart immediately behind them. "Come here," he said, waving Bob inwards. "I've been meaning to show you something."

Bob entered the cart, noting a silver-plated entrée dish, which Uncle Sam was uncovering to reveal a chainsaw.

"You remember when I told you we couldn't use electronic appliances in our show because we couldn't trust them?" Uncle Sam asked.

Bob nodded. "It was one of the first things you told me when I became your assistant."

Uncle Sam sprinkled a generous amount of Regenagent #32 on the device. "Well, as it turns out, the reason we had so many problems was because the souls weren't compliant enough."

"You've found a solution?"

"Yeah." Uncle Sam turned to Bob, watching him reflect on the chainsaw. "You make them complacent while they're still human."

Sam's hands bore down upon Bob. He struggled against the grip. The last thing Bob remembered before he lost all contact with his body was the sensation of worm-like appendages digging into his skull, groping for the surface of his scalp from the inside out. His eyes rolled back into his head as something stinging and hot obscured his vision. But he wasn't dead. He felt his mind course through a sharp, linked chain. His blood was a mixture of oil and gas, his heart, a two-cycle engine.

"Bob," Sam chuckled. "How do you feel?"

The saw buzzed with ferocity.

Uncle Sam picked up chainsaw Bob, found it compliant enough to control. "Relax. We'll be home soon."

Just then, the small caravan reverberated with Gary and the inanimals' war calls. Uncle Sam turned to address the media apparitions. "We have company!" he shouted. "Hold them off until I reach the factory!"

From the tent, a billowing cloud of shadows erupted, spreading across the landscape towards Gary and his inanimals. With them they carried weapons of graphite and shields of parchment, so they might rewrite history, revitalize movements and substantiate self-oppression.

At the edge of the storm, the forces caught sight of one another. Desks charged valiantly to flank media shadows that fought with utmost strength to reach Gary, the trophy of the inanimals' army. Against his will, Gary was enveloped by the bureaus, protected as if the queen in a game of chess. Liberty was inadvertently dragged to the outskirts, forced into battle by the very ebb and flow of the inanimals and their unorganized methods. Gary tried to direct them, but each had their own idea as to how battle was to be conducted. Yet, by chance, the bureaus' defensive maneuver found Gary less than twelve yards from Uncle Sam's convoy. "There it is men, er, inanimals!" he shouted, forgetting that his unit was no longer citizens, but clods of metal, wood and synthetic fabrics. "Keep moving!"

When his shouts were to no avail, Gary closed his eyes and willed his army in the direction of the convoy. The inanimals scurried accordingly, and the media shadows encircled them such that they now found themselves scrawling upon parchment at the rear and right side of the advance. The desks fanned out so the shadows could not penetrate, and Liberty was caught behind the front lines, able to meander through the crowd and back to Gary. "We're almost there!" he shouted. "One more push!" The inanimals surged towards the tent, hurtling Gary and Liberty to the forefront. "That's it!" Gary continued. "Hold them off once we get inside! Today, we'll have our answers!" The inanimals, could they have licked their lips to savor this moment, surely would have done so. Instead, they fought according to their leader's will as he and Liberty were hauled into Uncle Sam's caravan.

When they fell through the threshold, they were surprised to see the convoy void of life and silent, save the drone of a chainsaw exiting through the rear. They followed the sound to find Uncle Sam—rotting, liquid-like flesh pulling away from his skull—perched against his portable HAARP, kicking it in distress.

Noticing his pursuers, he picked up chainsaw Bob and threw it. Bob tore through Gary's midsection, but the wound reconstituted instantly. Still, the saw danced along the floor, threatening to harm Liberty.

"Stay behind me!" Gary warned.

"Have fun, kids," Uncle Sam said as he turned from them. "Play nice."

Liberty took a few steps back, watched the chainsaw spin chaotically. "Is it alive?" she asked.

Gary extracted his taser. "There's one way to find out." He waved it before the chainsaw. "Stop!" he insisted.

The machine slowed, backed into a corner.

"Sam's getting away!" Liberty screamed.

Gary turned to see Sam disappear in the storm. The taser fell as his concentration broke. Chainsaw Bob, noticing Gary was disarmed, gained its bearings and gave chase.

"Run!" Gary shouted.

Approaching the gates, Uncle Sam searched his pockets in hopes of procuring his vial of Regenagent #32. But the cap had shattered, the substance now leaking down the edge of his coat. He pried the gates open and ran inside, inadvertently dousing everything in his path with regenerative polyurethane.

Gary, Liberty and chainsaw Bob trailed behind, fighting their way through the encompassing storm to the factory's entrance.

"It's still behind us!" Liberty cried.

Gary, hands outstretched, opened the gate. "Come on!"

Liberty edged in only partially before becoming stuck. "I'm too big!"

"Turn over! I'll pull you through on your side!"

Chainsaw Bob was visible in the near distance.

"It's coming!" Liberty shouted.

Gary pulled with all of his strength, but she wouldn't budge.

"Leave me," she muttered hopelessly.

"I'm not leaving you." He paused in reflection. Her rear legs, they would have to come off. He started unscrewing them, trying to remember what he had learned years ago from Mr. Wakefield. "Right tight, left loose," he said to himself.

As Gary pulled the legs from her, chainsaw Bob was upon them. Gary tugged Liberty one last time, tearing her upholstery before hauling her through and closing the gate. He knelt before her, screwed her legs back on dutifully. "Are you ok?"

"I'll be fine."

"Alright. Let's find Sam."

* * *

Inside, they were greeted by the result of Uncle Sam's carelessness with the regenerative agent: machines of all sizes, all of which had been imbued with the souls of media apparitions and inanimals currently meeting their fate in battle. The machines tore from their casings in jealous pursuit of anything living. The very floor tiles shook to life, tripping Liberty as Gary rushed to confront Uncle Sam. They began smashing her in an orgy of self-destruction. Gary crawled back, pulled her from them and trudged onward until he saw a door in the distance slam shut, the coattail of Uncle Sam disappearing behind it.

* * *

Uncle Sam locked the door. He rummaged through the drawers in the room, finding only baby pins and pencils. He poured the last of the Regenagent on these objects and the large oak desk that contained them, willing them to confront anyone who should try to enter. The desk edged towards the door to block an intruder's way, while the pins and writing utensils stood erect, waiting for any sign of disturbance at the threshold.

* * *

When Gary rattled at the door, pins pooled through the keyhole to prevent him from entering, inadvertently unfastening the lock. Gary pushed Liberty behind him, fought against the scathing pins and found himself confronted by the oak desk. He lurched forward, hit it with all his might, but watched his hand become a puddle on the desk's surface and reconstitute moments later.

"Let me through!" he shouted, punching the desk again.

Uncle Sam laughed. "You still haven't figured it out have you, Gary? How do you expect to lead your precious inanimals to victory when you don't even have the will to control your own flaccid appendages?"

Gary could barely hear him over the sound of floor tiles, smashing again against his love. He thought about Mr. Wakefield, his parents and everyone else involved in the seemingly unfortunate streak of events that defined his very existence. Suddenly, it occurred to him. Until recently, he had never affected anyone or anything. Even before his transformation, he had been invisible, inconsequential, always like vitreous humor: transparent enough to be ignored in most circumstances, but thick enough to slow people down if forced to interact with him.

As a sense of hopelessness washed over him, he recalled the first time he held his whip, his first time raking shit and his night with Liberty, when his determination had allowed him to act, rather than be acted upon. He looked at the oak desk. "My fist is as solid as rock," he said. "My flesh is steel." He pulled back in one last attempt to move the object before him. And, when his fist came down, the desktop shattered. Kicking its remnants from the threshold, Gary rushed in.

He found an emaciated Uncle Sam, packing his legs behind a stack of dry ice.

"I guess that's the end of our cat and mouse pursuit," Sam said. He faltered momentarily as he tried to stand and called off the pins' assault. "I'm sorry you have to see me in such a state, but it's been my goal for some time."

Liberty entered behind Gary. "Uncle, what do you mean?" she conveyed telekinetically to Sam.

"I am illusion, remember—dream incarnate, a dream of something that never was and never will be. The hope of others is the only thing keeping me alive. Once the illusion of hope is shattered, I will disappear."

"You want to die?"

Uncle Sam nodded.

"Why didn't you just kill yourself," Liberty asked, "like mother?"

"I'm afraid it's not that simple. Once those who imagined us into existence share our graven images, we are no longer in control of our own lives. I have become a slave to the people. Your mother was fortunate enough to foresee the fate of our kind, and took her life before she could be imagined fully."

"So, this whole process was a suicide venture?" Gary asked.

"I had hoped you would take over for me," Uncle Sam replied. "Until the massacre in Philadelphia. Once the media ran with that story, the city forgot all about you and their precious little dreams, and I decided to take the operation nationwide." Sam walked to the window. "I thought that would be enough to finish me off. I should have known better. The hope of you and your little posse is keeping me alive. But not all is lost. Look! Your inanimals are losing the battle." He turned toward Gary and Liberty. His right ear, dangling from only a few strands of rotting skin, detached and fell to the floor.

Gary ran to the window and opened it. "Don't give up!"

The inanimals responded with a final push, but the shadows continued to overpower them.

Gary closed his eyes. *Please*, he thought. *Even in the face of death, hope.*

And as their brethren shattered around them under the force of the media shadows, several of the desks paused, reinvigorated by the abrupt return of their senses.

"What are you doing?" Uncle Sam cried. "Liberty, you're my niece! Stop him!" He slid down the wall, closed his eyes and, with all his power remaining, tried the impossible: to will the inanimals out of existence.

As Liberty watched her hunched and feeble uncle, focusing so intently with what little energy remained, she pitied him, though her empathy didn't outweigh her love for Gary.

Gary opened his eyes and, distracted by the scene below, failed to notice he rested against the windowsill with the aid of bone, sinew and flesh. Below, the inanimals used their sight to behold their new bodies, to feel one another with hands. The clamor of shattered wood and rending steel had been replaced with cries of joy.

Uncle Sam's color was returning. Deteriorating flesh coalesced around his nasal cavities, recreating features he had lost. He raised himself to the window. "No!" he shouted. "Do you know what this means? You bastards! I'll be stuck like this forever!"

Once-inanimals underwent metamorphosis and failed to notice the pleas of Uncle Sam above. Media shadows scribbled frantically, trying to divert the peoples' attention, but their efforts were in vain. The now-humans felt indebted to Gary, and were willing to listen to no other.

Liberty walked to their leader's side, cradled him in her cushions until armrests became arms, until the tattered holes in her covering became eyeless sockets. Gary returned the embrace. *Now all of you, dream*, he thought.

And they did, each imagining something different. Some dreamed of nostalgic things. Some hoped for a better future. Others simply reflected on what they were now doing— recreating their society and deities in the image of the people, one dream at a time.

ABOUT THE AUTHOR

A lifetime resident of Northern New York, Kirk Jones divides his time between writing, family, instructing English for the SUNY system, and playing guitar. He continues to work towards his PhD at Indiana University of Pennsylvania and feels tempted to "get meta" by mentioning the fact that he is referring to himself in the third person right now, but that seems pretty commonplace in author bios these days. Maybe if he spiced things up with some Bette Midler lyrics?

Bizarro books

CATALOG   SPRING 2010

Bizarro Books publishes under the following imprints:

www.rawdogscreamingpress.com

www.eraserheadpress.com

www.afterbirthbooks.com

www.swallowdownpress.com

For all your Bizarro needs visit:

WWW.BIZARROCENTRAL.COM

Introduce yourselves to the bizarro genre and all of its authors with the Bizarro Starter Kit series. Each volume features short novels and short stories by ten of the leading bizarro authors, designed to give you a perfect sampling of the genre for only $5 plus shipping.

BB-0X1
"The Bizarro Starter Kit"
(Orange)

Featuring D. Harlan Wilson, Carlton Mellick III, Jeremy Robert Johnson, Kevin L Donihe, Gina Ranalli, Andre Duza, Vincent W. Sakowski, Steve Beard, John Edward Lawson, and Bruce Taylor.

236 pages $5

BB-0X2
"The Bizarro Starter Kit"
(Blue)

Featuring Ray Fracalossy, Jeremy C. Shipp, Jordan Krall, Mykle Hansen, Andersen Prunty, Eckhard Gerdes, Bradley Sands, Steve Aylett, Christian TeBordo, and Tony Rauch.

244 pages $5

BB-001"The Kafka Effekt" D. Harlan Wilson - A collection of forty-four irreal short stories loosely written in the vein of Franz Kafka, with more than a pinch of William S. Burroughs sprinkled on top. **211 pages $14**

BB-002 "Satan Burger" Carlton Mellick III - The cult novel that put Carlton Mellick III on the map ... Six punks get jobs at a fast food restaurant owned by the devil in a city violently overpopulated by surreal alien cultures. **236 pages $14**

BB-003 "Some Things Are Better Left Unplugged" Vincent Sakwoski - Join The Man and his Nemesis, the obese tabby, for a nightmare roller coaster ride into this postmodern fantasy. **152 pages $10**

BB-004 "Shall We Gather At the Garden?" Kevin L Donihe - Donihe's Debut novel. Midgets take over the world, The Church of Lionel Richie vs. The Church of the Byrds, plant porn and more! **244 pages $14**

BB-005 "Razor Wire Pubic Hair" Carlton Mellick III - A genderless humandildo is purchased by a razor dominatrix and brought into her nightmarish world of bizarre sex and mutilation. **176 pages $11**

BB-006 "Stranger on the Loose" D. Harlan Wilson - The fiction of Wilson's 2nd collection is planted in the soil of normalcy, but what grows out of that soil is a dark, witty, otherworldly jungle... **228 pages $14**

BB-007 "The Baby Jesus Butt Plug" Carlton Mellick III - Using clones of the Baby Jesus for anal sex will be the hip sex fetish of the future. **92 pages $10**

BB-008 "Fishyfleshed" Carlton Mellick III - The world of the past is an illogical flatland lacking in dimension and color, a sick-scape of crispy squid people wandering the desert for no apparent reason. **260 pages $14**

BB-009 **"Dead Bitch Army" Andre Duza** - Step into a world filled with racist teenagers, cannibals, 100 warped Uncle Sams, automobiles with razor-sharp teeth, living graffiti, and a pissed-off zombie bitch out for revenge. **344 pages $16**

BB-010 **"The Menstruating Mall" Carlton Mellick III** - "The Breakfast Club meets Chopping Mall as directed by David Lynch." - Brian Keene **212 pages $12**

BB-011 **"Angel Dust Apocalypse" Jeremy Robert Johnson** - Meth-heads, man-made monsters, and murderous Neo-Nazis. "Seriously amazing short stories..." - Chuck Palahniuk, author of Fight Club **184 pages $11**

BB-012 **"Ocean of Lard" Kevin L Donihe / Carlton Mellick III** - A parody of those old Choose Your Own Adventure kid's books about some very odd pirates sailing on a sea made of animal fat. **176 pages $12**

BB-013 **"Last Burn in Hell" John Edward Lawson** - From his lurid angst-affair with a lesbian music diva to his ascendance as unlikely pop icon the one constant for Kenrick Brimley, official state prison gigolo, is he's got no clue what he's doing. **172 pages $14**

BB-014 **"Tangerinephant" Kevin Dole 2** - TV-obsessed aliens have abducted Michael Tangerinephant in this bizarro combination of science fiction, satire, and surrealism. **164 pages $11**

BB-015 **"Foop!" Chris Genoa** - Strange happenings are going on at Dactyl, Inc, the world's first and only time travel tourism company.

"A surreal pie in the face!" - Christopher Moore **300 pages $14**

BB-016 **"Spider Pie" Alyssa Sturgill** - A one-way trip down a rabbit hole inhabited by sexual deviants and friendly monsters, fairytale beginnings and hideous endings. **104 pages $11**

BB-017 "The Unauthorized Woman" Efrem Emerson - Enter the world of the inner freak, a landscape populated by the pre-dead and morticioners, by cockroaches and 300-lb robots. **104 pages $11**

BB-018 "Fugue XXIX" Forrest Aguirre - Tales from the fringe of speculative literary fiction where innovative minds dream up the future's uncharted territories while mining forgotten treasures of the past. **220 pages $16**

BB-019 "Pocket Full of Loose Razorblades" John Edward Lawson - A collection of dark bizarro stories. From a giant rectum to a foot-fungus factory to a girl with a biforked tongue. **190 pages $13**

BB-020 "Punk Land" Carlton Mellick III - In the punk version of Heaven, the anarchist utopia is threatened by corporate fascism and only Goblin, Mortician's sperm, and a blue-mohawked female assassin named Shark Girl can stop them. **284 pages $15**

BB-021 "Pseudo-City" D. Harlan Wilson - Pseudo-City exposes what waits in the bathroom stall, under the manhole cover and in the corporate boardroom, all in a way that can only be described as mind-bogglingly irreal. **220 pages $16**

BB-022 "Kafka's Uncle and Other Strange Tales" Bruce Taylor - Anslenot and his giant tarantula (tormentor? fri-end?) wander a desecrated world in this novel and collection of stories from Mr. Magic Realism Himself. **348 pages $17**

BB-023 "Sex and Death In Television Town" Carlton Mellick III - In the old west, a gang of hermaphrodite gunslingers take refuge from a demon plague in Telos: a town where its citizens have televisions instead of heads. **184 pages $12**

BB-024 "It Came From Below The Belt" Bradley Sands - What can Grover Goldstein do when his severed, sentient penis forces him to return to high school and help it win the presidential election? **204 pages $13**

BB-025 "Sick: An Anthology of Illness" John Lawson, editor - These Sick stories are horrendous and hilarious dissections of creative minds on the scalpel's edge. **296 pages $16**

BB-026 "Tempting Disaster" John Lawson, editor - A shocking and alluring anthology from the fringe that examines our culture's obsession with taboos. **260 pages $16**

BB-027 "Siren Promised" Jeremy Robert Johnson & Alan M Clark - Nominated for the Bram Stoker Award. A potent mix of bad drugs, bad dreams, brutal bad guys, and surreal/incredible art by Alan M. Clark. **190 pages $13**

BB-028 "Chemical Gardens" Gina Ranalli - Ro and punk band Green is the Enemy find Kreepkins, a surfer-dude warlock, a vengeful demon, and a Metal Priestess in their way as they try to escape an underground nightmare. **188 pages $13**

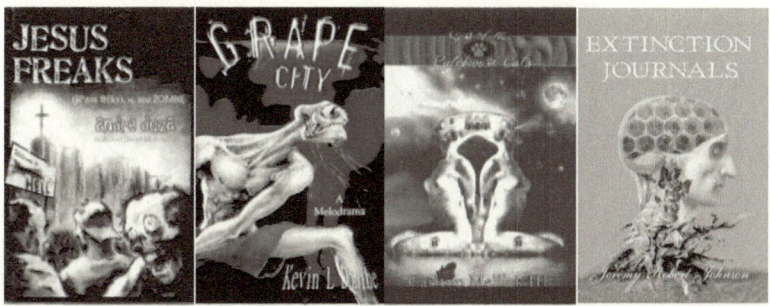

BB-029 "Jesus Freaks" Andre Duza - For God so loved the world that he gave his only two begotten sons… and a few million zombies. **400 pages $16**

BB-030 "Grape City" Kevin L. Donihe - More Donihe-style comedic bizarro about a demon named Charles who is forced to work a minimum wage job on Earth after Hell goes out of business. **108 pages $10**

BB-031"Sea of the Patchwork Cats" Carlton Mellick III - A quiet dreamlike tale set in the ashes of the human race. For Mellick enthusiasts who also adore The Twilight Zone. **112 pages $10**

BB-032 "Extinction Journals" Jeremy Robert Johnson - An uncanny voyage across a newly nuclear America where one man must confront the problems associated with loneliness, insane dieties, radiation, love, and an ever-evolving cockroach suit with a mind of its own. **104 pages $10**

BB-033 "Meat Puppet Cabaret" Steve Beard - At last! The secret connection between Jack the Ripper and Princess Diana's death revealed! **240 pages $16 / $30**

BB-034 "The Greatest Fucking Moment in Sports" Kevin L. Donihe - In the tradition of the surreal anti-sitcom Get A Life comes a tale of triumph and agape love from the master of comedic bizarro. **108 pages $10**

BB-035 "The Troublesome Amputee" John Edward Lawson - Disturbing verse from a man who truly believes nothing is sacred and intends to prove it. **104 pages $9**

BB-036 "Deity" Vic Mudd - God (who doesn't like to be called "God") comes down to a typical, suburban, Ohio family for a little vacation—but it doesn't turn out to be as relaxing as He had hoped it would be… **168 pages $12**

  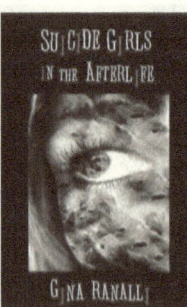 

BB-037 "The Haunted Vagina" Carlton Mellick III - It's difficult to love a woman whose vagina is a gateway to the world of the dead. **132 pages $10**

BB-038 "Tales from the Vinegar Wasteland" Ray Fracalossy - Witness: a man is slowly losing his face, a neighbor who periodically screams out for no apparent reason, and a house with a room that doesn't actually exist. **240 pages $14**

BB-039 "Suicide Girls in the Afterlife" Gina Ranalli - After Pogue commits suicide, she unexpectedly finds herself an unwilling "guest" at a hotel in the Afterlife, where she meets a group of bizarre characters, including a goth Satan, a hippie Jesus, and an alien-human hybrid. **100 pages $9**

BB-040 "And Your Point Is?" Steve Aylett - In this follow-up to LINT multiple authors provide critical commentary and essays about Jeff Lint's mind-bending literature. **104 pages $11**

BB-041 "Not Quite One of the Boys" Vincent Sakowski - While drug-dealer Maxi drinks with Dante in purgatory, God and Satan play a little tri-level chess and do a little bargaining over his business partner, Vinnie, who is still left on earth. **220 pages $14**

BB-042 "Teeth and Tongue Landscape" Carlton Mellick III - On a planet made out of meat, a socially-obsessive monophobic man tries to find his place amongst the strange creatures and communities that he comes across. **110 pages $10**

BB-043 "War Slut" Carlton Mellick III - Part "1984," part "Waiting for Godot," and part action horror video game adaptation of John Carpenter's "The Thing." **116 pages $10**

BB-044 "All Encompassing Trip" Nicole Del Sesto - In a world where coffee is no longer available, the only television shows are reality TV re-runs, and the animals are talking back, Nikki, Amber and a singing Coyote in a do-rag are out to restore the light   **308 pages $15**

BB-045 "Dr. Identity" D. Harlan Wilson - Follow the Dystopian Duo on a killing spree of epic proportions through the irreal postcapitalist city of Bliptown where time ticks sideways, artificial Bug-Eyed Monsters punish citizens for consumer-capitalist lethargy, and ultraviolence is as essential as a daily multivitamin. **208 pages $15**

BB-046 "The Million-Year Centipede" Eckhard Gerdes - Wakelin, frontman for 'The Hinge,' wrote a poem so prophetic that to ignore it dooms a person to drown in blood. **130 pages $12**

BB-047 "Sausagey Santa" Carlton Mellick III - A bizarro Christmas tale featuring Santa as a piratey mutant with a body made of sausages. 124 pages $10

BB-048 "Misadventures in a Thumbnail Universe" Vincent Sakowski - Dive deep into the surreal and satirical realms of neo-classical Blender Fiction, filled with television shoes and flesh-filled skies. **120 pages $10**

BB-049 **"Vacation" Jeremy C. Shipp** - Blueblood Bernard Johnson leaved his boring life behind to go on The Vacation, a year-long corporate sponsored odyssey. But instead of seeing the world, Bernard is captured by terrorists, becomes a key figure in secret drug wars, and, worse, doesn't once miss his secure American Dream. **160 pages $14**

BB-051 **"13 Thorns" Gina Ranalli** - Thirteen tales of twisted, bizarro horror. **240 pages $13**

BB-050 **"Discouraging at Best" John Edward Lawson** - A collection where the absurdity of the mundane expands exponentially creating a tidal wave that sweeps reason away. For those who enjoy satire, bizarro, or a good old-fashioned slap to the senses. **208 pages $15**

BB-052 **"Better Ways of Being Dead" Christian TeBordo** - In this class, the students have to keep one palm down on the table at all times, and listen to lectures about a panda who speaks Chinese. **216 pages $14**

BB-053 **"Ballad of a Slow Poisoner" Andrew Goldfarb** Millford Mutterwurst sat down on a Tuesday to take his afternoon tea, and made the unpleasant discovery that his elbows were becoming flatter. **128 pages $10**

BB-054 **"Wall of Kiss" Gina Ranalli** - A woman... A wall... Sometimes love blooms in the strangest of places. **108 pages $9**

BB-055 **"HELP! A Bear is Eating Me" Mykle Hansen** - The bizarro, heartwarming, magical tale of poor planning, hubris and severe blood loss... **150 pages $11**

BB-056 **"Piecemeal June" Jordan Krall** - A man falls in love with a living sex doll, but with love comes danger when her creator comes after her with crab-squid assassins. **90 pages $9**

BB-057 **"Laredo" Tony Rauch** - Dreamlike, surreal stories by Tony Rauch. **180 pages $12**

BB-058 **"The Overwhelming Urge" Andersen Prunty** - A collection of bizarro tales by Andersen Prunty. **150 pages $11**

BB-059 **"Adolf in Wonderland" Carlton Mellick III** - A dreamlike adventure that takes a young descendant of Adolf Hitler's design and sends him down the rabbit hole into a world of imperfection and disorder. **180 pages $11**

BB-060 **"Super Cell Anemia" Duncan B. Barlow** - "Unrelentingly bizarre and mysterious, unsettling in all the right ways..." - Brian Evenson. **180 pages $12**

BB-061 **"Ultra Fuckers" Carlton Mellick III** - Absurdist suburban horror about a couple who enter an upper middle class gated community but can't find their way out. **108 pages $9**

BB-062 **"House of Houses" Kevin L. Donihe** - An odd man wants to marry his house. Unfortunately, all of the houses in the world collapse at the same time in the Great House Holocaust. Now he must travel to House Heaven to find his departed fiancee. **172 pages $11**

BB-063 **"Necro Sex Machine" Andre Duza** - The Dead Bitch returns in this follow-up to the bizarro zombie epic Dead Bitch Army. **400 pages $16**

BB-064 **"Squid Pulp Blues" Jordan Krall** - In these three bizarro-noir novellas, the reader is thrown into a world of murderers, drugs made from squid parts, deformed gun-toting veterans, and a mischievous apocalyptic donkey. **204 pages $12**

BB-065 "Jack and Mr. Grin" Andersen Prunty - "When Mr. Grin calls you can hear a smile in his voice. Not a warm and friendly smile, but the kind that seizes your spine in fear. You don't need to pay your phone bill to hear it. That smile is in every line of Prunty's prose." - Tom Bradley. **208 pages $12**

BB-066 "Cybernetrix" Carlton Mellick III - What would you do if your normal everyday world was slowly mutating into the video game world from Tron? **212 pages $12**

BB-067 "Lemur" Tom Bradley - Spencer Sproul is a would-be serial-killing bus boy who can't manage to murder, injure, or even scare anybody. However, there are other ways to do damage to far more people and do it legally... **120 pages $12**

BB-068 "Cocoon of Terror" Jason Earls - Decapitated corpses...a sculpture of terror...Zelian's masterpiece, his Cocoon of Terror, will trigger a supernatural disaster for everyone on Earth. **196 pages $14**

BB-069 "Mother Puncher" Gina Ranalli - The world has become tragically over-populated and now the government strongly opposes procreation. Ed is employed by the government as a mother-puncher. He doesn't relish his job, but he knows it has to be done and he knows he's the best one to do it. **120 pages $9**

BB-070 "My Landlady the Lobotomist" Eckhard Gerdes - The brains of past tenants line the shelves of my boarding house, soaking in a mysterious elixir. One more slip-up and the landlady might just add my frontal lobe to her collection. **116 pages $12**

BB-071 "CPR for Dummies" Mickey Z. - This hilarious freakshow at the world's end is the fragmented, sobering debut novel by acclaimed nonfiction author Mickey Z. **216 pages $14**

BB-072 "Zerostrata" Andersen Prunty - Hansel Nothing lives in a tree house, suffers from memory loss, has a very eccentric family, and falls in love with a woman who runs naked through the woods every night. **144 pages $11**

BB-073 "The Egg Man" Carlton Mellick III - It is a world where humans reproduce like insects. Children are the property of corporations, and having an enormous ten-foot brain implanted into your skull is a grotesque sexual fetish. Mellick's industrial urban dystopia is one of his darkest and grittiest to date. **184 pages $11**

BB-074 "Shark Hunting in Paradise Garden" Cameron Pierce - A group of strange humanoid religious fanatics travel back in time to the Garden of Eden to discover it is invested with hundreds of giant flying maneating sharks. **150 pages $10**

BB-075 "Apeshit" Carlton Mellick III - Friday the 13th meets Visitor Q. Six hipster teens go to a cabin in the woods inhabited by a deformed killer. An incredibly fucked-up parody of B-horror movies with a bizarro slant. **192 pages $12**

BB-076 "Rampaging Fuckers of Everything on the Crazy Shitting Planet of the Vomit At smosphere" Mykle Hansen - 3 bizarro satires. Monster Cocks, Journey to the Center of Agnes Cuddlebottom, and Crazy Shitting Planet. **228 pages $12**

BB-077 "The Kissing Bug" Daniel Scott Buck - In the tradition of Roald Dahl, Tim Burton, and Edward Gorey, comes this bizarro anti-war children's story about a bohemian conenose kissing bug who falls in love with a human woman. **116 pages $10**

BB-078 "MachoPoni" Lotus Rose - It's My Little Pony... *Bizarro* style! A long time ago Poniworld was split in two. On one side of the Jagged Line is the Pastel Kingdom, a magical land of music, parties, and positivity. On the other side of the Jagged Line is Dark Kingdom inhabited by an army of undead ponies. **148 pages $11**

BB-079 "The Faggiest Vampire" Carlton Mellick III - A Roald Dahl-esque children's story about two faggy vampires who partake in a mustache competition to find out which one is truly the faggiest. **104 pages $10**

BB-080 "Sky Tongues" Gina Ranalli - The autobiography of Sky Tongues, the biracial hermaphrodite actress with tongues for fingers. Follow her strange life story as she rises from freak to fame. **204 pages $12**

BB-081 **"Washer Mouth" Kevin L. Donihe** - A washing machine becomes human and pursues his dream of meeting his favorite soap opera star. **244 pages $11**

BB-082 **"Shatnerquake" Jeff Burk** - All of the characters ever played by William Shatner are suddenly sucked into our world. Their mission: hunt down and destroy the real William Shatner. **100 pages $10**

BB-083 **"The Cannibals of Candyland" Carlton Mellick III** - There exists a race of cannibals that are made of candy. They live in an underground world made out of candy. One man has dedicated his life to killing them all. **170 pages $11**

BB-084 **"Slub Glub in the Weird World of the Weeping Willows"**
Andrew Goldfarb - The charming tale of a blue glob named Slub Glub who helps the weeping willows whose tears are flooding the earth. There are also hyenas, ghosts, and a voodoo priest **100 pages $10**

BB-085 **"Super Fetus" Adam Pepper** - Try to abort this fetus and he'll kick your ass! **104 pages $10**

BB-086 **"Fistful of Feet" Jordan Krall** - A bizarro tribute to spaghetti westerns, featuring Cthulhu-worshipping Indians, a woman with four feet, a crazed gunman who is obsessed with sucking on candy, Syphilis-ridden mutants, sexually transmitted tattoos, and a house devoted to the freakiest fetishes. **228 pages $12**

BB-087 **"Ass Goblins of Auschwitz" Cameron Pierce** - It's Monty Python meets Nazi exploitation in a surreal nightmare as can only be imagined by Bizarro author Cameron Pierce. **104 pages $10**

BB-088 **"Silent Weapons for Quiet Wars" Cody Goodfellow** - "This is high-end psychological surrealist horror meets bottom-feeding low-life crime in a techno-thrilling science fiction world full of Lovecraft and magic..." -John Skipp **212 pages $12**

ORDER FORM

TITLES	QTY	PRICE	TOTAL

Please make checks and moneyorders payable to ROSE O'KEEFE / BIZARRO BOOKS in U.S. funds only. Please don't send bad checks! Allow 2-6 weeks for delivery. International orders may take longer. If you'd like to pay online via PAYPAL.COM, send payments to publisher@eraserheadpress.com.

SHIPPING: US ORDERS - $2 for the first book, $1 for each additional book. For priority shipping, add an additional $4. INT'L ORDERS - $5 for the first book, $3 for each additional book. Add an additional $5 per book for global priority shipping.

Send payment to:

BIZARRO BOOKS
 C/O Rose O'Keefe
 205 NE Bryant
 Portland, OR 97211

Address

City   State   Zip

Email   Phone

www.ingramcontent.com/pod-product-compliance
Lightning Source LLC
Chambersburg PA
CBHW020730250626
47155CB00006B/2241